You won't want to miss any of the memorable characters in this newest series by bestselling author Lass Small. While each of THE KEEPERS OF TEXAS *books stands on its own, the continuing saga of the Keeper family and ranch will surely keep you coming back for more!*

You met Rip and Lu in *Taken by a Texan* (Desire #1137). And they are back again, and prepared to stir up some trouble for Lu's brother....

ANDREW PARSONS: He was the houseguest from hell! The arrogant, rugged Texan just wouldn't leave the Keeper ranch, nor would he learn any manners. As a last resort, Mrs. Keeper called in some favors and asked for the much-needed help of family friend...

JOANN MURRAY: It was said she could tame any man, though she hadn't yet let one into her bed. Until she met a certain cantankerous cowboy. Was that love in the air...or just frustration, say for another Texan bachelor....

TOM KEEPER: The heir to the Keeper ranch just seemed to meet woman after woman that he couldn't have. Well, he was bound and determined not to fall in love again. But it wouldn't be that way for long, not if a certain set of parents have anything to say about it....

The Keeper family saga will continue in September with *The Lone Texan,* Lass Small's fiftieth book for Silhouette! Don't miss any of the fun and romance you're sure to find with *THE KEEPERS OF TEXAS.*

Dear Reader,

This month, Silhouette Desire celebrates sensuality. All six steamy novels perfectly describe those unique pleasures that gratify our senses, like *seeing* the lean body of a cowboy at work, *smelling* his earthy scent, *tasting* his kiss…and *hearing* him say, "I love you."

Feast your eyes on June's MAN OF THE MONTH, the tall, dark and incredibly handsome single father of four in beloved author Barbara Boswell's *That Marriageable Man!* In bestselling author Lass Small's continuing series, THE KEEPERS OF TEXAS, a feisty lady does her best to tame a reckless cowboy and he winds up unleashing *her* wild side in *The Hard-To-Tame Texan*. And a dating service guarantees delivery of a husband-to-be in *Non-Refundable Groom* by ultrasexy writer Patty Salier.

Plus, Modean Moon unfolds the rags-to-riches story of an honorable lawman who fulfills a sudden socialite's deepest secret desire in *Overnight Heiress*. In Catherine Lanigan's *Montana Bride,* a bachelor hero introduces love and passion to a beautiful virgin. And a rugged cowboy saves a jilted lady in *The Cowboy Who Came in From the Cold* by Pamela Macaluso.

These six passionate stories are sure to leave you tingling… and anticipating next month's sensuous selections. Enjoy!

Regards,

Melissa Senate

Melissa Senate
Senior Editor
Silhouette Books

Please address questions and book requests to:
Silhouette Reader Service
U.S.: 3010 Walden Ave., P.O. Box 1325, Buffalo, NY 14269
Canadian: P.O. Box 609, Fort Erie, Ont. L2A 5X3

LASS SMALL
THE HARD-TO-TAME TEXAN

SILHOUETTE *Desire*
Published by Silhouette Books
America's Publisher of Contemporary Romance

SILHOUETTE BOOKS

ISBN 0-373-76148-1

THE HARD-TO-TAME TEXAN

Copyright © 1998 by Lass Small

This edition published by arrangement with Harlequin Books S.A.

® and TM are trademarks of Harlequin Books S.A., used under license.
Trademarks indicated with ® are registered in the United States Patent
and Trademark Office, the Canadian Trade Marks Office and in other
countries.

Printed in U.S.A.

Books by Lass Small

Silhouette Desire

Silhouette Romance

Silhouette Yours Truly

Silhouette Books

*Lambert Series
†Fabulous Brown Brothers
‡ The Keepers of Texas

LASS SMALL

finds living on this planet at this time a fascinating experience. People are amazing. She thinks that to be a teller of tales of people, places and things is absolutely marvelous.

One

Prologue

Back, some time ago, Andrew Parsons had intruded onto the TEXAS tableland of the Keepers. He just clipped the herd-restraining fence and entered where he chose. He didn't mend the rip he'd caused in the barbwire.

As Andrew had ridden along, his horse had been silently shot from some awesome, silent distance. At the time, Andrew didn't even know the horse had been shot. He thought it had a heart attack or something similar.

After Andrew's leg had been hopelessly trapped under his dead horse for just past two days, it was Andrew's dog who searched for help. The lost dog had eventually been seen by Tom Keeper.

Tom had used his cell phone to contact the pilots to see where the earnest dog wanted to go and why. And the pilots did find the trapped Andrew.

Rescued, Andrew was in the hospital for some time. One of the ranch pilots, Rip, had taken care of Andrew's dog. And Rip had taken the dog to see his master. That was how Rip had met Andrew's logical, normal, alluring sister, Lu Parsons.

Now Andrew was to be released from the area hospital, out there on the TEXAS tableland. However, Andrew—the obsolete man—was perfectly comfortable, in hospital, living as he chose, being cared for by others.

He slept in the daytime and visited with the nurses and watched TV in the night. His time was askew; the hospital was tolerant. People are people. Some are strange.

The time came when Andrew was able to walk. He could eat by himself and he could shower alone. He was capable of sharing his time with other people. The doctors scolded the staff. Andrew was not to be pampered, the room in the hospital was needed for other patients.

That was said sternly. It was all vocally underlined. No one mentioned the night nurses had spoiled him.

Andrew did not want to leave the hospital. It was a haven. When told he should go, he'd said, "Not yet."

The staff was adamant, "There are others who need the space in the hospital." They told Andrew he could use his leg, which was healing. "It is time for you to leave us," they told him.

Andrew was irritated and turned stubborn. He repeated, "Not yet."

So what was to be done with him? He was alone. There was no place for him to go. His father refused him.

Having been unable to reach any agreement with Andrew's family in Houston, the staff at the hospital contacted those who had brought the pilgrim to them. They talked to the Keepers who lived out and beyond. Their land seemed endless.

The Keepers recommended the hospital contact the Parsons family again and gave them another phone number. Unfortunately the hospital person contacted Mr. Parsons who was very odd. And, with hostility, he declined sharing stress with his son.

The hospital crew became terse.

Eventually, it was the Keepers who accepted the burden of the pilgrim.

Andrew paid none of his hospital bills.

His sister, Lu, who was by then living with the Keepers' pilot Rip Morris, insisted that the Parsons were responsible and must take the bill. And before that was done, she did some telephone talking with her father in Houston. The father was a man very similar to his son.

His father did pay the bill. Mr. Parsons was not gracious. He simply sent the check to the hospital. Then his daughter let go of his throat. Holding a throat with dug-in fingernails, over a long-distance phone, is not easy.

So with the reluctantly courteous invitation of the Keepers, Andrew Parsons was taken from the hospital

and moved into the big house at the Keepers' place.
That place was where Keepers had been for something like five centuries. It hadn't been easy.

As the Keepers had gone along through time, they
had coped with many problem people. That's why
their house was so large. The family had secret access
to stairs and corridors. They could avoid just about
anyone. With that security, they offered an interim
shelter to Andrew Parsons.

Andrew kindly accepted that he was a guest of the
Keepers'. He had no concern at all. He knew his ac-
ceptance was a gift to the Keepers.

So the Keepers again were reminded of their name,
and it was they who finally, reluctantly volunteered
to become the keepers of Andrew. And Andrew very
easily accepted the care as due him.

He allowed the staff to clean his room and to bring
him meals and care for him. He expected such conduct, all for him. He did not hesitate to ring the bell
for attention.

As Andrew healed, more fully, the staff became
restless. They had other things to do and other people
for whom to care. The crew began to revolt.

It was Tom Keeper's mother who went to see Andrew in his room. He was reading, sitting with his
back to the window. With the knock, he said, "Come
in." And as Mrs. Keeper entered, he smiled and
falsely pretended to move to stand.

Mrs. Keeper stood just inside the room and smiled.
"You're much better. Tonight you may come down
for dinner." She ignored his protest and continued,

"Tom and his brother Sam will come by for you and guide you down."

"I'm really not yet—"

But Mrs. Keeper was leaving the room as she said, "Dinner is at six." And she was…gone.

That was blunt enough.

Andrew phoned the doctor. It was a house phone and he called long distance. He gave the phone number. The Keepers would pay.

The nurse said, "The doctor is with a patient. How can we help?"

Identifying himself, Andrew said, "They're trying to get me to walk downstairs to dinner!"

The nurse flipped through Andrew's medical records. Then she said, "You're capable. Do it." And she hung up.

Andrew was furious. He paced and gestured and breathed and was livid! He didn't want to be sucked in by others' rules. He had his own. It was to allow himself to do as *he* chose.

So Andrew didn't go down to dinner with Tom and his brother Sam. Andrew had locked the door. When someone knocked at five 'til six, Andrew said through the door, "I'm not well enough to go down yet."

Tom said, "Okay."

Andrew said through the door, "Send my supper up to me."

There was no reply.

No one came.

Andrew went without dinner. He was furious.

About ten that night there was another knock at his door. With the sound, Andrew was in a fury. He snarled, "The door is not locked." He'd assumed he'd *finally* be getting his dinner. And he turned deadly eyes on the door.

His sister, Lu, came inside with a smile. "You're still up?"

"I've not yet had dinner...not even supper."

"Oh."

"Go down to the kitchen and get me something to eat." It was not a request. It was an order.

Lu watched her brother thoughtfully. She understood exactly why Mrs. Keeper was doing as she was. Lu said kindly, "The kitchen is closed." She patted her pockets and said, "I do have a caramel." She held it out to her brother.

He snatched it with steely fury and threw it against the wall as he retorted, "That isn't enough."

She considered him. "Well, then, drink a whole lot of water and fool your stomach." She turned and opened the door. Over her shoulder she advised, "Practice walking and come down for breakfast in the morning."

As he drew in an indignant breath, she went out and closed the door behind her.

Andrew was infuriated. No one was doing as he said. He was abandoned. He tore the bed apart and shoved furniture around. He was not quiet. With all the chaos finished, he sat in one chair and panted with anger and exhaustion.

Finally, he phoned down to the servants to ask for someone to come straighten his room and bring him some food. No one replied to the ring. He let it ring a hundred times. He could be dying. Who cared?

He considered that. Who would care? His father? He was too concerned with himself. His mother? She never took her amused eyes from his father. His siblings? All were self-centered. None cared two hoots in hell about him. They were just like his sister, Lu.

He looked at his silent dog who watched him thoughtfully.

His Buddy.

Would Buddy abandon him, too?

So Andrew made up his bed. It wasn't because he regretted tearing it apart, it was because he had to sleep in it, and no one had come to tidy his room. He was bitter. He sat sourly.

The dog sighed rather obviously. Rather enduringly.

He said to the dog, "When I'm stronger, we'll leave and go our own way by ourselves."

The dog watched him and did not respond or wag his tail or anything. It was as if Buddy understood every word said and was opposed to such nonsense.

With that intrusive awareness, Andrew remembered how the dog had looked around and moved his head when they were out on the tableland. And belatedly, Andrew realized that Buddy had never been sure out there. He'd been watchful and careful and listening. Hmmm.

It was interesting that Andrew had known, all through that time, that the dog was uneasy, and he had ignored the animal's alertness. He'd thought it'd been rabbits.

If it had been rabbits, the dog would have investigated it. Whatever had rattled the dog, out on the tableland, it hadn't been anything close. The long, silent path of that great bullet that had killed the horse had been proof of the distance.

So Andrew went to bed that night without any supper. Neither had the dog been fed. Andrew forgot that part. He hadn't taken the dog down to where the dogs were fed. Since he hadn't eaten any supper, it didn't occur to him to see to it that the dog did.

Buddy went into the bathroom and drank a lot of water. That was, of course, out of the toilet. Then the dog came back into the bedroom, curled down in a corner and slept. He was used to such times. Most of those times, he had been hungry because Andrew had forgotten to feed him.

When the man had remembered, the dog was eager and the man only chided the dog for being rude. Just the fact that Andrew had more dog food than was needed ought to have been some clue. Actually, Andrew only thought about himself.

So the man and dog slept that night with rumbling, complaining stomachs. It was especially strange that Andrew endured the hunger. He could have gone downstairs anytime in the night and found something in the kitchen. He was just mind-bogglingly stubborn.

So that hungry morning, Buddy considered the man more closely. He didn't sneak looks, he observed.

Finally, the man said to the dog, "You can go out by yourself. I'll open the door. You can leave."

To Andrew's surprise, the dog got up and went to the door and stood there waiting for it to be opened.

The knob was high, he could not reach it. He looked at the man.

Andrew's temper flared. He went to the door and snatched it open...and the dog was gone! Just like that.

Such an "escape" made Andrew blink. He found he was still holding the door open. He closed it gently, firmly. The dog would not get back inside unless he scratched on the panel.

Andrew smiled. If the dog scratched to get inside, the door would be marked. Okay. He'd just wait to go down to the second breakfast. He'd just see who had control of the door.

Buddy was not back by the time Andrew heard the subtle, ringing sound for the second breakfast. And it was obvious to Andrew that if he wanted anything to eat, he would have to go downstairs, right then.

As he opened the door, he looked down both sides of the hall and saw only a few people who paid no attention to him at all.

For a man who had once been paid to be on TV to tell tales of his adventures, it was very strange not to be noticed by those people there.

They treated him as if he was—average.

The use of the word *average* caused Andrew to be pensive. He would despise being labeled as average. He was an adventurer. An explorer.

Andrew arrived in the dining room as the tables were being cleared. Those doing that, nodded cheerfully to the lagging person who was almost too late for the meal. They offered serving plates that had been almost cleared off, but there were tidbits still available.

The laggard guest was so hungry that he didn't mind taking the last of things. That made him seem ordinary to those clearing the tables. To them, he was an ordinary man who'd overslept. He was just from the hospital, wasn't he? And his timetable might be a bit odd for a while, but he was healing quite well. There was no reason to indulge him.

The crew was tolerant. Someone brought fresh orange juice; another brought in fresh coffee. They all spoke to him. He nodded rather formally. They assumed he was starving and therefore hadn't the time to chat. They didn't mind.

One said, "Your dog came down and ate, then he asked to go out. Since you allowed him from your room, that way, we figured you didn't mind if he went out by himself."

Coldly, Andrew replied, "He is a stranger here."

Another said in passing, "We're keeping an eye on him."

Andrew's eyes lowered in irritation. How could they keep an eye on a dog that was outside? Buddy would be lost. Well, maybe not. He did pretty well by himself.

Sullenly, Andrew rubbed his stomach and felt isolated clear out there, alone, with no entourage. Being alone and traveling was very different from being in a large house where he wasn't known. They were treating him as if he was like everyone else. How rude.

He ate enough to live on without gorging himself

with food. He felt like gorging, but he knew better than to be that stupid. He did not speak or smile as any reply to those around. No one had asked if they could speak. He had not asked it of them. They were just help. He did not need to tolerate any familiarity from anyone.

He lay his napkin next to his plate and pushed his chair back to rise.

One of the crew asked, "Enough? We have some lovely fruit cobbler."

Andrew looked coldly at the man and replied rudely, "No."

"Good. Then I get it!" He laughed easily. Then he explained, "We flipped a penny. If you didn't want it, I won!"

But Andrew didn't even wait to hear what was said by who all. He'd walked out.

One of the crew said, "I'd guess...and it's just a guess, you know, but I'll bet some really elegant, feisty female just ditched him."

Another considered and then nodded. "That could well be. He's in a snit."

But somebody else said, "He could just be a selfish bastard."

Since they all laughed, and did know him slightly, the fact that Andrew Parsons *was* one, was soon known through all the Keeper help.

The house crew had already been told that Andrew Parsons was capable of walking, of eating downstairs. He could shower alone and shave himself.

While he'd slept days at the hospital, and been

awake all night watching TV and visiting with the nurses, he could now walk well enough to get around on his own.

The more he did that—walking—the better his leg would be.

He selected a cane from a collection the Keepers had in a cylinder at the bottom of the stairs, and he gently, perfectly used it.

Then the staff was further cautioned that Andrew Parsons was just about completely healed. He was capable of dressing alone and of walking by himself. The selected cane was all drama. Ignore it.

The staff was told that Andrew could share his time with other people. He was not to be pampered. That was underlined. At the hospital, the nurses were so kind they had just about ruined him. At the Keepers' place, he was to take care of himself with minimal attention or assistance.

The crew could assist him only if he fell and could not manage to get up by himself—they paused and then aided him—only after he'd tried three times.

Andrew was not ignored. Everyone talked to him. But no one…helped him. No one arranged his plate or cut his meat or…fetched things for him.

With such obvious lack of attention, Andrew was as sulky as a spoiled child.

Of course, when any of the crew went from the Keeper Place into town, they did manage to report progress to the hospital crews. And at first, they chided the people at the hospital for corrupting Andrew Parsons so carelessly.

But those at the hospital retorted, "He was that way when we got him!"

The Keeper crew chided, "He is rock-bottom spoiled."

The hospital staff admitted, "Well, we *did* let him sleep when he wanted, and he just got his days and nights mixed up a little." They figured that admission would be enough.

The Keeper bunch said, "We'd never in the world allow something that dumb out there at our place."

Since that hospital was where any harmed person was taken, the medical crew *then* said, "He was spoiled before you all ever got ahold of him. His parents didn't even come to see him. We figured they'd abandoned him, he was so difficult. Then we found out the grandparents had been in a terrible wreck and lingered for a long old time. His daddy is now weird about hospitals."

One of the ranch crew said softly, "Ahhhh. I don't think I knew that. Parsons wasn't that harmed."

Thoughtfully the ranch crew shifted as they looked at the vast space around as if to be sure that it was still there. Then they mentioned, "He is strange. Most outdoor people really hate being trapped inside."

So the hospital crew shared, "Readjusting him will be a challenge to you all. Good luck." They were leaving the crew, but they all hesitated and one cautioned earnestly, "Don't send him back to us."

"You gotta know how much the Keepers've put into that pile of bricks you all call a 'hospital'?"

"Careful. You might need us. We can attach legs backwards."

"Uh-oh. Uhhhhh… We was just warning you all about that strange Parsons person. You could get him back without wanting him again."

And the intern shook his head. "Don't fret about us. Our Admittance Office is cold and sly. We only get people who actually need us. We wouldn't have taken him, but he had a bad leg. That got him inside. Then the nurses didn't care which shift got him. It don't make no nevermind to them."

One of the ranch crew asked, "Where you from again?"

The intern started out: "Uhhhh. How come you want to know?"

"You're getting the swing of talking TEXAN pretty good now."

And another of the hospital crew mentioned, "It's the sunshine and the food. Any man and most women are susceptible to being TEXAN. It's in the climate. And other people around and about talk thataway. It's catching…like a cold."

One of the ranch crew was fascinated. "I hadn't ever been told that. Do you suppose it's the *climate* that makes us thisaway?"

"Wouldn't be a-tall surprised."

So being gossi—communicators, the critical words about Andrew Parsons's conduct did slide along all around the area. It was just a surprise that it didn't go on to other states and foreign countries.

They finally figured the reason the word hadn't spread on beyond was because the TEXANS are not gossips and only mention odd conduct to good, closed-mouthed friends. They smiled at one another.

It was good to be able to trust other people. They were all TEXAN, born and bred.

So Andrew Parsons had been discarded and ignored. At the Keeper Place, he was where he could recover. He had a room. His sister, Lu, visited him. He assumed she was still at the hospice, in town, near the hospital. He hadn't been interested enough in her to find out what she was now doing, or why she hadn't gone on back to Houston?

And the thought came to Andrew that she was still around! He was out of hospital. There was no need for her to be there! Why was she still hanging around? Hmmmm.

But when he went to the dining area, he didn't see his sister anywhere. Had she left? How strange. No farewell? Well, it didn't bother him at all. She was useless anyway. She'd insisted the family pay his hospital bills.

The Parsons had done that. It was only right that they did. It had been their son and his horse that had been shot. No one had mentioned replacing his horse. That would come...the time when he could mention his dead horse.

What had become of his faithful dog?

Using the cane, Andrew ventured carefully onto the porch and whistled the call for the dog. It did not appear. Where was he? Not that Andrew cared much one way or the other. To whistle for the dog was an excuse to get out on the terrace. He didn't want to appear physically ready for trodding around the area.

After his horse had been shot, Andrew hadn't felt

any urge to again go out onto the land…at all. So it was no surprise that right away he went back inside the Keepers' house. No one was anywhere around. There was no one to entertain him.

That didn't mean someone for him to watch. It meant someone who would ask him questions and then listen to what he had to say.

Of course.

All of the world was anxious to know what reply Andrew Parsons would give. He'd wondered why he hadn't been asked back to the Oklahoma town's television station. He asked. They said there had been no response…at all.

When Andrew demurred, they searched for and found and gave him one postcard that had said, "Good gravy, man, can't you find anything else for us bed-bound guys?"

Andrew had said the obvious: That was only one person's opinion. But he hadn't gotten through to even one of the blank heads confronting him.

One had said, "Do you know how many people have been on the places where you've ridden?"

Andrew had replied, "Think of the people who have walked in the path of others?"

"Most of those paths have been made by celebrated, intelligent travelers. Most of that time is past. There is nothing in your presentation that is either new or different."

"Then…why did you accept my interview?"

"Desperation. We are cured of it. We are changing the concept."

"How will I fit in?"

"No way. Not here. Good luck."

And they'd escorted him out of the place...and closed their door on his heels.

What was it about adventure that had faltered? And his mind gave him the view of loaded cars on interstate highways. People traveling. A whole lot didn't even look at the countryside. They read. Played games. Slept. The driver watched the road and noted the speed and maneuvering.

Times had changed when Andrew hadn't noticed. He was a throwback to another time. Out of it? How strange.

If he was obsolete, then why did people go to museums? And he remembered being a child when an old cousin came to visit with them. He didn't really visit. He read the paper and watched TV. Andrew's own mother invited the elderly cousin to go to the museum, which was one of the eleven best in the country.

The old cousin said, "I've seen a museum."

He indicated that if you've seen anything once, it was enough. It wouldn't change. Museums did.

Think of the people who go to see the paintings and stand and just stare at them, absorbing the lights and shadows, the colors, the genius of it.

There are people who have such paintings or photos or drawings in their homes. They smile at them or stand and allow their eyes to draw the drawings into their brains and feel fulfilled.

Andrew really wasn't such a person. He was not a viewer. He felt he, himself, was enough for any audience. He was unique and precious and worthwhile. He was there for them to regard and admire.

Yeah. Sure.

Two

Late that evening, Mrs. Keeper was sitting on the wide stool before her vanity mirror. She rolled her hair onto small wire rounds and pinned them with odd, bendable, plastic hairpins. She looked as if she'd just landed from some faraway planet.

Her husband came over and sat on his side of the stool, which had been custom-made for that very reason. His legs were on either side of her and his arms were around her body, nicely, but his hands were not in control. He asked, "What are we going to do about Andrew?"

She sighed with his "we" comment because what he actually meant was: What was *she* going to do about Andrew.

She fiddled with the lengths of hair tightly wound up in all those plastic doodads. She mentioned, "I've called Mark's daughter JoAnn?'' That's the TEXAS questioning do-you-understand statement. ''She's coming to see us and she's going to smooth Andrew...out.''

With his eyes closed, Mr. Keeper's hands were exploring his wife's front chest. He mentioned, ''Women terrify me.''

She turned her head slightly and looked at him loftily over her shoulder from under hooded eyes. She said, ''—you are terrified—with reason. You brought me out to this raw place and, even now, you expect me to adjust.''

''You've done that very well.''

''Hah!''

Indignant, he reminded her, ''I let you go in to San Antone twice a year to shop.''

''You go along and shake your head over anything I put on!''

''That's how well you make a rag look when it's on your body. I'll not have you wearing rags.''

She was patient. ''If they look good on me, then they're not rags.''

And *he* said, ''Oh,'' as if he'd learned something.

''Why are you clutching my breasts? Do you think you're going to fall off the stool? You had it made so that you wouldn't.''

''I'm being helpful.'' He breathed on the back of her neck and his hands cupped her breasts closely. ''It's nice you have two. One for each hand. No quarreling of hands. Each is content.''

She sighed with some drama. ''You're groping me again.''

That shocked him for her lack of understanding. "No, no, no! I'm keeping them from jiggling!"

"How kind." Then she told her husband, "I can't think of anything else to do with him." She didn't even have to say the name of Andrew Parsons.

So her husband solved everything. "Let's take him back out on the tableland and just dump him. We could shoot a horse to put on top of him."

"Not any of our horses."

He accused, "You're picky."

She moved her mouth around as if she was searching out food caught in her teeth, then she sighed impatiently, "He's human."

"No! Really?"

And they were then silent. He relished her body and neck. She went on winding up every damned little curl.

She mentioned, "Your parents will be here in about three more days."

Her husband chuckled in his throat.

"Why do you laugh?"

"How young they are. My daddy's just barely twenty years older. My momma is only twenty-one years older than you. They really hurried. I was born exactly nine months after they were married!"

"—and your daddy was in Europe, fighting in that awful war."

"Yeah. He didn't think he'd get back."

"I'm glad he did."

"Me, too." Then he looked at her in the mirror, and they smiled at each other. But he told her, "I have only one eye."

She was patient. He did that all the time. She told him, "Move your head over to your right. You will see that you have two eyes."

He did that and exclaimed in lousy surprise, "Glory be!"

He continued sitting astraddle her hips, and he gently moved his evening beard on her shoulder giving her erotic goose bumps. But he was very diligently holding her breasts to keep them from wiggling.

When she finally finished winding her hair and had captured all of the curls on her head, he asked, "Ready?"

"For what?"

"Me."

"Don't joggle my hair."

He chided, "I never have! The hair on your head isn't one of your sexual lures."

"I'll take out the pins."

"Naw. I'd never notice."

"You just like my body."

"I like you, your body, your essence, the way you laugh, and that sneaky little smile when you want me."

She was indignant. "I have *never* wanted you. I'm just a used sex slave."

"Wow." He laughed. "How come you clutch me and writhe and move around and gasp."

"Endurance." But she licked her smile with a naughty tongue and her eyes were wicked.

So two days later JoAnn Murray drove up to the Keepers' door with two suitcases, which she judiciously left in her car. She was redheaded. That meant that she was independent. Redheads always are.

Redheaded people had to endure a lot of discussion about the color of body hair, and teasing. That sort of thing solidifies their character. They're unique and they live as they damn well choose.

After greeting Mrs. Keeper, JoAnn said, "Mother ruthlessly sent me here to cope with your obvious problem and get rid of him. I am skilled in getting rid of males. Mother loves you. This will clear her books with your kindness in helping her. She underlined that. You are to agree with her clean record now, before I do anything about this leech you've acquired."

Mrs. Keeper replied, "Well, hello, JoAnn. How *is* your dear mother?"

"Dramatically relieved you've asked me to do this and not asked her. She says she's too old to deal with young men anymore. She only watches them in the Soaps."

"Your mother is dear to me."

JoAnn was tolerant. She advised in a mature manner, "We all have our moments. Tell me about this male burden who made you send out an S.O.S. for the first time since mama's known you in college. She is so curious."

As the two women of different ages talked, they entered the house and went into a side room downstairs. There, they were served tea as Mrs. Keeper had directed the kitchen crew before JoAnn's arrival.

JoAnn sipped some, then more and closed her eyes as she tilted her head and smiled. "Ahhh. It's perfect...as usual."

Mrs. Keeper didn't make tea. She slept with Mr. Keeper and that was about all she did. Of course, the crew was her choosing.

If someone had made lousy tea, Mrs. Keeper would have isolated them with their cook until the newcomer knew exactly how to make tea. No one was ever fired. They were turned over to the head cook, or the head butler or the head gardener, and on occasion to her and was instructed more widely.

Educating and adjusting newcomers was the same with everybody who was on the Keeper place. It included everyone who was around, involved in cooking, housecleaning, barns, animals, plowing, flying, whatever.

So the tea was perfect. The servers had hesitated on the other side of the door and watched. Mrs. Keeper sipped the tea and looked at it and she smiled. That was like a pat on the head for the watchers and they went back to the kitchen.

Mrs. Keeper inquired, "Are those in your family all well?"

"Fine. This tea is perfect."

"We have a wonderful crew."

See? Mrs. Keeper was kind. So she then said, "What are we to do about this Andrew Parsons?"

"Don't worry. I'm here. I'll get rid of him for you."

"Well," hesitated Mrs. Keeper, "I really think he needs to be...uh...restructured. It would be unkind for us to just pitch him onto a sand dune. Isolated again. He needs to fit into some portion of society better.''

JoAnn was thoughtful. "I don't believe I've ever done anything like that. I believe you've contacted the wrong person for this. I'm a rejecter." JoAnn then smiled kindly to soften the blow for Mrs. Keeper. People tended to be thataway with Mrs. Keeper. She appeared to be quite fragile.

Mrs. Keeper tasted the word, "Re-ject-er. Push away. Discard.''

"Yep.''

"I shall have to find someone else." She sighed in a fragile manner. "But in the time that will take, could you begin by teaching Mr. Parsons that he will very soon be in the twenty-first century? He needs to realize that he is at the very *end* of the twentieth?''

"Well...''

Mrs. Keeper elaborated to explain herself. "Andrew needs to look forward to stepping over into the next century. He hasn't even been in this one. He's of another time.''

She sighed gently before she went on: "He believes that his adventures are all a surprise for the rest of us. Either actually telling of where he's been, or being on TV, that time, or writing of it in books. He does not realize that we have mostly already looked all around this planet, the moon, and now Mars. There is no new place for Andrew on this entire earth. On horseback, he is a throwback.''

Mrs. Keeper paused and considered JoAnn. "While I search for someone to upgrade him, do you think you could endure at least allowing him to talk to you? He is quite isolated here.''

JoAnn shrugged. ''I haven't anything at all on my calendar. It would give me something to do.''

''I really appreciate your help. I shall try to be quick in finding someone else to help him. Do what you can.''

JoAnn sighed. ''Okay. I'll get my luggage.''

''Let Tom. He has nothing to do, and it would please him to help you.''

Nothing to *do?* Tom's own mother assumed *Tom* had nothing to *do?* He had no *time,* at *all!*

At that moment, Tom was at Rip's plane getting ready to board when his cellular phone burped. He was surprised. People very *rarely* called him! He looked at Rip and said, ''My phone!''

Rip observed Tom with curiosity and said, ''Yeah.'' A beep was a beep. So—

So Tom pulled the phone into reality and lifted it as he said, ''Tom.''

And his mother said, ''Darling, I need you here.''

''Yes.'' Then Tom refolded his phone and put it back into his pocket as he said, ''Mother needs me. Let me go with you later?''

''Yeah. Meanwhile, I'll go on out…looking.''

''You need someone else with you. Ask Ben or Wilkie?''

''Okay.''

''Thanks. Be careful.''

''Yeah.''

* * *

So Tom's Jeep pulled up to the door of the Keeper place. And there was his mother and... Why, it was JoAnn! His mother looked okay. She wasn't stressed. JoAnn grinned.

His mother said to Tom, "We need your muscles to get JoAnn's luggage into the house. She's going to have the room just down the hall from us. There on the left. That guest room."

Tom blinked. He'd been called back...to move...luggage? There was a whole, entire house crew for such. His mother was going into the winky-dink time?

Tom said, "Okay." And he went the ten steps to JoAnn's car and effortlessly lifted out her two bags. He carried them to the door and found his mother waiting for him to open the door for them.

Okay.

He put down the suitcases and escorted the ladies back inside. Then he retrieved JoAnn's luggage.

As he reentered the house, he asked JoAnn, "You been visiting?"

"I got here just a while ago. We've been talking and drinking—tea."

His eyes twinkled and he moved his lips so his grin was interrupted.

JoAnn said, "So you're out here and working on the place?"

"Just another ranch hand." He exchanged an amused glance. He hadn't seen JoAnn for some time. She looked pretty good to his eyes. How about her showing up with luggage! How come?

"You on the circuit?" Then he bit his lip. She was

about thirty. She might be embarrassed by her visiting...with him there. Was his momma waving her under his nose? He looked at her again and thought, okay.

But his mother was saying rather sternly, "I asked JoAnn to come in order to bring Andrew up to time. He believes he's the only one who has even been on the tableland."

Tom scoffed, "He's a pilgrim."

"Yes." His mother sighed and walked farther down the cool hallway.

JoAnn followed. She had stiffened a bit with Tom's impulsive inquiry if she was back on the circuit. She had never *been* on the circuit! She was a current, independent woman and she didn't *need* the circuit to find a willing man! With her daddy's money, she didn't *need* to go looking for *any* man!

She became somewhat aloof.

Redheads can get hostile real quick like. Tom sighed inside his body and began to verbally tape over his stupidity. He said, "That's some automobile you got out there."

"It's a dream."

He asked, "Take me for a ride this evening?"

JoAnn replied vaguely, "I'll see."

She gave him a very independent look. Or was it... a...rejecting one? Well, if it was, it shouldn't surprise Tom any. He'd missed so many perfect women who'd gotten married off to somebody else, that he wouldn't be at all surprised to be dumped by this one just about immediately.

Andrew Parsons came carefully down the hall with

a cane helping his left leg walk. He was lonely and bored. He'd heard female talk. So he snooped. He smiled courteously and lowered his head in a minimal bow as he apparently meant to go on by them.

Mrs. Keeper said, "Good morning, Andrew. Allow me to introduce you to my new guest."

That red hair— Andrew's eyes sparkled. He stopped with courteous interest, his eyes on the red-headed one. He hadn't even noticed Tom. Andrew had no real interest in Tom anyway and found him unsuitable because Tom had never been at all interested in Andrew's adventures.

The *reason* Tom wasn't interested was because he'd been out on that tableland how many thousands of times? To search, to herd, to just be alone out there. That had been when he first had his own horse. He'd gone out to help watch a herd stay in the area allotted to them in the wet times when the grasses were lush.

Tom went out on the tableland to find steers that had avoided being rounded up. To find calves that cows had dropped and discarded. And just recently, to look for whoever it was out there who'd shot that great bullet and knocked Andrew's horse over…dead.

Tom had observed the changings of the land in the gentle, subtle seasons. The tableland was fragile and beautiful. He took pleasure in the looking around and loved the land.

Tom had little endurance with the pilgrim who saw the tableland as bleak and useless, craggy and water-less. Andrew hadn't looked well enough. There were springs out yonder, if a man knew where to look.

And nobody who lived around there was ever going to give away the secrets of the hidden places.

So now a cranky Tom inquired of the pilgrim, "When you clipped our fences, did you see any of our No Trespassing signs?" Now that was about the most blatant comment Tom could make to the pilgrim.

His mother was appalled and stood straighter.

Andrew replied kindly, "I didn't see any signs. Perhaps you should have larger ones?"

Tom looked levelly at the pilgrim and said, "But you did see that the area was fenced. That should have been some sort of clue it *is* private land?"

His mother put her hand around a portion of Tom's arm and subtly shook it, indicating that he was being rude enough and to cut it out.

Tom turned his head slowly and just looked stonily at his mother.

She inquired, "Will you be here for lunch?"

Tom replied, "No." He just walked on off, but he tilted his hat barely enough to JoAnn, as he went out the door, got into his Jeep and left.

It was probably Tom's doing exactly that which caught JoAnn's attention, causing her to blink. So Tom wasn't as wimpy as she'd thought. How interesting.

She looked at Andrew. She considered him. Mrs. Keeper had indoctrinated JoAnn on exactly what all Andrew had done. JoAnn wondered how in the world Andrew had ever gotten along in this current time. He was obviously interested in her. She tended to attract male attention. It was boringly her red hair that lured men. They always wanted to know if her hair was red...everywhere?

The very idea of such interest exasperated JoAnn.

So she looked at Mrs. Keeper who was kind and gentle, and her mother's best friend. JoAnn had to complete her effort to help Mrs. Keeper. She could not say, "Well, so long," and just leave. She had to do as her mother had requested.

Since JoAnn didn't give one hoot in hell about this obsolete creature, called Andrew, she just might catch his logical attention and straighten him out. Maybe. He was probably more mature— He was how old? Probably about forty. A little old to be adjusted by someone her age. He probably would not listen to her. She'd see.

She looked back at Andrew. He was sliding his eyes down her body. That was about what every male did. To her, it was irritating. So basic. She wondered if there was any man around anywhere who would consider her mind first. Most of them never noticed that she had a brain. The males almost all thought she was a wingy-ding.

They just wanted to see the silken hairs on her body and find if they were the color of the hair on her head. They were most earnest about that. She had never been snared by such a dummy. That's why she was still single.

Men were single-minded and rather limited. Uh...not Tom. It had been a surprise that he'd exited as he had. She would give him another look over.

But in the meantime, she had to do something

about that lost-in-time person, Andrew Parsons, who didn't know which side was up.

While JoAnn was thinking that, Andrew was secure in the fact that she was taken with him. How that came about, God only knows, but Andrew smiled at her kindly.

Like the nurses at the hospital, women tended to be lured by Andrew. He understood that was so…and accepted it. He sighed gently, but he was very pleased.

Buddy, who had been Andrew's dog, had escaped and gone over to Rip's house. He knew the house because Rip had kept him there nights when Andrew had been hospitalized.

This time, Buddy had abandoned Andrew. It had taken some time for Buddy to realize Andrew *used* a dog or a person. The human male was extensively spoiled. Buddy had been loyal and endured. But not being fed last night had been the crowning blow. Once too often. He'd gone hungry too many times. Buddy was through caring for the selfish Andrew.

So the dog had gone to Rip's house.

At Rip's house, Buddy just went through the dog door and barked once to let them know he was back.

Andrew's sister, Lu, came into the living room at Rip's house. She smiled at the dog. "So you've come home."

The dog understood the words which people never know dogs knew, and he smiled. He laughed. His tongue panted and his smile was wide.

Lu asked, "How'd you get away?"

The dog looked at the dog door and back at Lu. He'd given her a reply.

Lu asked, "Are you here to visit?"

The dog went under the table and lay down. That was to indicate he was hiding there, and she wasn't to tell anyone she'd seen him.

She didn't catch on at all. She squatted down and asked, "Why are you under there? Are you hiding?"

Buddy came out, sure she understood his plight and that she was on his side. He smiled at her.

She laughed and said, "I'm glad to see you, too. Come into the kitchen while I finish the dishes. Look at my hands! Who would ever believe I'm a Parsons?"

The dog gave a discreet, low bark as he told her she was perfect.

She asked, "You're hungry? You can't be! You're teasing me. We only feed our dogs in the morning and again in the evening. You're not to get a lunch, too!"

The dog laughed. She wasn't too sharp but she was kind.

She said, "Rip will be here for lunch. I just *might* give you a little taste...if you *promise* not to blab. Okay?"

The dog had to walk around a little with his head down. But he thought she was hilarious.

Rip came inside the house in a hurry. He ignored the dog and just took Lu against his body as he kissed her. She wiggled against him to get even closer and blushed and kissed him back.

Even though the dog pranced and barked to get in

on the greeting, neither person was aware of it. They clutched each other, kissed and—not letting go of each other—they stumbled into the bedroom. And at the last minute, Rip closed the bedroom door.

So Buddy was in the hall. He was closed out. He could hear the rustle of clothing, Lu's soft laughter, and the creek of the bed. Buddy felt sorry for the people. Their mating was so complicated. With dogs, it was easier.

Three

For Andrew Parsons, the days were too long and the
nights were even longer. He was bored out of his
gourd, but he didn't know of any other place where
he wanted to be.

Actually, he'd had no response from any of those
places that he'd contacted as a haven. He'd contacted
a good many places while in hospital where he had
been recovering from his injuries.

There were some places that had regretted with a
brief but polite rejection, but there were those that had
never replied. Either way, it had been demeaning.

Andrew wondered if Mrs. Keeper was going to oust
him from the Keepers' place. Would she?

He avoided confronting her.

He did not want to go home.

His father was simply ridiculous. He was such a

burden on Andrew's mother. His father needed his mother by him all the while. Such a leech.

Andrew did not think of himself as a leech. Not at all. Never. He was a jewel of a guest. He realized that. The fact that he was there heightened the caliber of any place.

He had been educated abroad in one of England's exclusive, private schools. Those who'd been students were brain heads and rather strange. If one did not know of their particular interest, he had been rejected by the students.

Andrew had learned to speak as they did and discarded the TEXAS speech. They laughed at his accent and word choice. His speaking as they did, had made no impression at all.

It had been a long, hard time, but he had learned to be aloof. He knew his value.

So he had been the only student who was interested in the States, he had been terribly homesick, and one elderly, bumbling man taught Andrew in that pioneer field of TEXAS. Unfortunately, everything the old man knew had occurred long ago.

They didn't know of anything current about the United States. They hadn't even thought doing so could be important.

However, no one at the Keeper place paid Andrew much mind. Of course, everyone was civil. They greeted Andrew and nodded across a room, but no one ever sat down with him and asked him questions. Nor did they ask his opinion. No one ever asked his point of view on any subject.

Andrew had all this long-ago knowledge of the

States stacked up inside himself, and no one was curious enough to ask him a question. How strange is such a careless, rejective world.

Of course, Andrew didn't approach any other person. He didn't offer anything at all to anyone. He waited to be approached. He was tolerant of the people who did not know of history or of the makings of the world. He had his own opinions, his own ideas. He could give people another view.

They didn't ask.

He didn't offer.

The reason he never started a subject was not that he wasn't outgoing. He had been. But too often the listener got up, excused himself and…left. —or one just walked on off to start with. Escaped?

Andrew felt that people needed to know basics. They needed to know who and how and why things were as they'd been. Everybody seemed to think current knowledge was enough.

They put it on the internet.

How can people build on things unless they know basics? How did people live before there were ovens? How did they cope with weather before there were chimneys? How did they now handle cars when there'd been just horses?

It was basic knowledge.

Andrew didn't know any better. It was probably his father's fault. Mr. Andrew Parsons Sr. was such a fool. With Andrew knowing his father was how he was made, his eldest son would flinch at the very thought of being made by such a man.

It was only astonishing that Andrew's grandfather

allowed his son, Andrew's father, a portion of his estate. Andrew would have nothing when his father had used that all up. His father was not stable.

Andrew's father had seen a droll movie about plastics when he was vulnerable. He didn't have the humor to understand the film. He *believed* in plastics. He owned stock in plastics. He was caught in something that could never last. And he would shrivel away along with his inherited money.

Andrew's father needed to understand. He needed to listen to his son about the beginnings. Unfortunately, it appeared that every other person in this world was hell-bent on going on beyond plastics to breathing synthetics.

There are people who just never understand the world is moving along—without them. Oddly enough, Andrew was such a person.

He had all those past things stacked up in his mind, and no one gave a hoot in hell about any of it.

How strange that the busy, distracted and kind Mina Keeper knew all that about Andrew Parsons. And it was she who told JoAnn how to smooth Andrew into understanding this finishing twentieth century.

"He is a throwback to another time," Mina Keeper mentioned needlessly. "We need to upgrade him somewhat. How about you working on that first, JoAnn. You do that while I'm trying to find someone else who can help him."

JoAnn said, "Okay. I'll try. Don't expect anything.

He's in the clasp of his own regard and probably won't listen.''

Very kindly, Mina Keeper mentioned, ''You need to make him think he's teaching *you* all that stuff.''

JoAnn licked her lips thoughtfully as she mentioned, ''Stuff'' in a manner that was an echo of Mrs. Keeper. It was an important communication about which she wasn't entirely sure.

Rather drolly, Mina Keeper said, ''He's not in step with other people. We need to upgrade him enough so that he understands the current times.''

''Oh. Well. I think I can help with that. I shall try.'' Then she asked, ''Have you found someone to take my place as yet?''

''Not yet. I'm searching.''

''Well, get on it as soon as you can, or I might louse up this outdated person who is named a rather current Andrew.''

Mina mentioned, ''We had a long-ago president named Andrew Jackson.''

''Compared to Andrew Parsons, Andrew Jackson is almost current.''

That made Mina Keeper laugh.

So Mina saved that to tell her husband that night as she was again winding up her hair in little swirls and trapping them just so.

Sprawled on the bed, John Keeper said, ''Compared to Andrew Parsons, Andrew Jackson was modern.'' And John added, ''Has it ever occurred to you how fast this world has progressed in just the last one hundred years? My grandmother went from horse and buggy to watching the moon landing on TV, for crying out loud!''

Winding her hair, Mina replied, "I know."

"Andrew has a long way to come up to normal. Let's get rid of him."

Mina turned and looked at her husband. He was watching her.

She told him, "Darling, we have to help this poor person advance until he can join in with other people of this time."

John rejected that. "He's a throwback, there's no question. How do you expect to do anything about him?"

"I've turned him over to JoAnn for now. She'll help until I find someone who can instruct him better."

John raised his head to look at her with direction. "Let's get rid of him. Out of sight, out of mind."

"He is our guest. We cannot just turn him out. We must see to it that he can fit in."

She got up and went to him with her hair half-done. She sat by him and lay back near him. She said, "You're a king."

"Yeah."

"It's because of you that I willingly live out in this beyond. I love you, John."

"Ah, Mina, my love."

So the discussion about Andrew was lost for that night.

It was the next day that John's odd parents arrived. Bart Keeper had given the ranch to his son John. Bart and Alice traveled. They stayed in odd places and found odd things and sent gifts home. No one really knew what to do with the gifts.

Under Mina's subtle guidance, the family finally voted on a museum-type room. That way, they could display the things sent to them by the parents/grandparents. And they had a viewing for the parents/grandparents when they arrived back at the ranch.

Getting things out of papers and displaying and then putting them away had been a nuisance. This way it all looked as if the children and grandchildren appreciated the things gathered in such respect.

Feather dusters were a godsend. The gifts could be dusted quickly if the grandparents came in a surprise. Fortunately, they mostly called ahead.

Since the family had had money for so many years, everything bought for looking at it was just a waste of good cash. John was tempted to sell the stuff, but his wife, Mina, had said, "Not yet."

Alice Keeper was a good deal like her daughter-in-law, Mina. Before the senior couple left again, it was Alice who coached JoAnn in what all she should do about the laggard Andrew Parsons.

So JoAnn changed into boots and trousers with a big TEXAS hat and went in search of Andrew. She did find him and sat down in a chair across from him.

His reply to her greeting was a stiff almost imperceptible nod.

After a silence, she said to the settling tire-iron who lived around their necks, "Tell me about the Russians who share their space station."

Bruskly minimizing, Andrew retorted, "The station is obsolete. It will probably fall the entire way. It will probably hit in one of our oceans."

She countered, "We go up there to the Russian station. Our people share the station."

"If the Russians rejected us, the space station wouldn't be stable."

She was rather astonished he was even that current. "How do you know that?"

"They aren't us."

JoAnn shrugged and put out her hands. "They had it built before we've managed one. We have no station in space."

With some endurance, Andrew told her, "We are planning to land on Mars."

Now that was astonishing for JoAnn to hear from Andrew. It was *current!* She didn't know enough about it to continue the conversation. So she asked, "Would you go to Mars?"

And he replied a finalized type of, "No."

So, to continue this remarkable conversation, she asked, "Why not?"

Impatiently, Andrew replied, "There are no people there."

"How do you know that?"

"No water." He frowned a little and looked around for some escape as he breathed harshly...

So JoAnn asked, "Where would you like to go?"

He said in a deadly way, "Away from here."

"Why would you want to leave here?"

He looked directly at JoAnn and said, "It's boring."

"Do you play cards?"

He enunciated it specifically, "No."

"Do you ride...horses?"

With caustic rudeness, he mentioned, "My leg."

She was well aware that he was enduring her. He was rude and would rather not be accosted by her, but he had no choice. She asked, "Where would you like to go if you could go anywhere in the world?" That old saw of desperation.

He looked at her. He considered. He looked away. He could think of no other place. He said, "Why don't you run along home to your mother?"

And *she* said, "I'm bored. Talk to me."

He was caught. He did understand boredom and he did understand being ignored. He looked at her and saw her patience. She just might listen to him and be impressed. She wasn't too dumb. And he might practice communicating with her to ease other times of chat with current people.

He asked, "What do you want to know?" Actually, he didn't give one hoot in hell about her. His voice was not interested. *He* was not interested. He was enduring her. It was obvious.

Being thirty and not thirteen, she almost smiled, but she asked with interest, "If you had lived two hundred years ago and had the choice to come to this time, would you have done that?"

Oddly enough, no one had ever asked him that question. He was somewhat irritated. She didn't ask him what was important then, she asked if he would have wanted to live then.

Andrew said, "I would have come here."

And rudely, basically pushing the nomad, she replied, "Just tampons would have convinced me to come to this time."

Andrew looked at her with some shock that she would speak of such. To a man? He opened his mouth to set her down and—

"Would you want to wear the clothes of that time?" Then she added, "What would you have done about condoms?"

He thought she was vulgar. Tampons and condoms. What else did she harbor in her mind? So he asked, "What else would you take back just two hundred years?" He asked it rather snidely.

She grinned. "That's easy. Cars, dishwashers." She gestured one hand in circles. "—telephones, X-ray, air-conditioning, medical upgrading, dental equipment—"

"You are a modern woman."

"You bet."

"What...man...would you take with you?"

She surprised him with an immediate reply, "A current plumber. He could fix the water supply and figure out an automatic clothes washer."

And he inquired, "What would you think of a current telescope?"

"To look at the stars? Naw. If I could take anything that big, it would be a radio hookup."

Oddly that time-man asked, "What about a boat motor?"

She dismissed it all, "Men can row and there are sails."

"What sort of stove would you have?"

"Any fire would do. Matches were available at that time."

"A—refrigerator?"

JoAnn discarded it aside with one hand. "Not all that necessary."

"Why not?"

"In the summer we would eat from the garden, and in winter, we would use a box outside for the fridge. My grandmother mentioned ancestors pulling a box of food up into a tree away from animals in winter. The wooden box served as a fridge. That happened in Ohio."

Andrew's attention was lured. He didn't have family memories. He was caught by hers. "Which side of the family told you these stories?"

"My mother's side. They wrote of everyday things and saved letters. They knitted socks and shawls. They didn't have a sewing machine, but heard tell of such. I would want one."

"So you sew?"

"Heavens, no. But in that situation, I would learn. They had parties. They wore costumes. They had fun."

"I never thought of that time as being...fun. I thought it was all work."

JoAnn thoughtfully replied, "I suppose it is attitude that matters." She looked at him, then added, "—even now." That was close enough.

Andrew gave her a quick look. Was she saying *his* attitude was wrong? But she was smiling a little. Probably remembering other things her forebears had done.

And Andrew was touched. He had never known of his own ancestors. How would it be to know them? To know *of* them. What they had done and how they had lived. What had been important to them?

She said, "When my great-grandmother was in the Great Depression, and my grandmother was a child, the great-grandmother typed addresses on penny post-cards to pay for a typewriter. She gave piano lessons until she could pay for a piano. She had been raised playing a piano. She had learned to type on a strange looking, early typewriter. It must have been an interesting time."

He agreed. With a rather abstract nod, he said, "Like the computer now." Then he said, "I don't know about my kin that far back."

"You ought to look them up in the genealogical library. Then perhaps you could find a cousin or two who had been given letters or stories about your family."

"Have you?"

"I know my people."

He observed her.

That was the only way she could think of it. He was curious about her family...and now his own. Would he search them out? It would be interesting. How many would want to deal with Andrew Parsons? That would be even more interesting.

She interrupted his self thoughts saying, "Let's go exercise your leg."

Andrew had an instant brain flash picture of her sitting on his stomach and pulling his harmed leg around. His lips parted as he—

And she said, "I'm restless. Let's walk."

Andrew looked at her and saw her. She was a person. Another person. As he was one, so was she. And she was desperate for something to do. She was not someone who sat and visited. She wanted something that was interesting.

It occurred to him that, to her, he was not interesting! That was a startling knowledge! And it was only then that he realized his mother loved him. Now that was a shock! His mother listened as she watched him.

And he realized that not only did she love him, she had missed him when he was away. Her letters had come weekly. She had written all the news. He had not replied. He'd hated being there in England, away from home, unlike anyone around him. Rejected.

Not only had the other students rejected him, but his mo— It had been his father who'd wanted him gone. Yeah. So that was why he'd been sent away. His father was such a wimp that he'd wanted all his wife's attentions.

But his father had written to him.

Andrew had read the plump letters "...do your best." in scorn. He'd burned his father's letters.

He had kept all those his mother had sent.

And walking beside the guest whose name he didn't recall, Andrew understood that his father probably was jealous of him. Or— He was such a loner that he thought Andrew would grow and expand if he was given another environment.

Andrew had hated being away from TEXAS. He had hated being away from his own people. It had been terrible for him to cope with another environment.

He was too different in all ways—from dress to speech. His heart had shriveled. He could have been with those who were his own kind. He hadn't needed to be pressed against the rejection in England.

And he wondered for the first time if the other kids had wanted to be there in school. Some had. They all had much in common. They knew the games, the words, the formal clothing. Only he was a stupid tagalong.

He could have gone to TEXAS University. His family still put the state first. It wasn't really the University of TEXAS, it was right out there, TEXAS University.

Andrew looked around. There was nothing in sight. A trifle alarmed, he asked the female, "Where are we?"

"There's a spring over yonder. Let's see if there are any prints of animals. Do you know prints?"

"Not likely." How strange to hear the TEXAS comment come from his own lips. He smiled.

There was a mottled blue enamel cup hanging from a big nail impaled in a crooked branch. He took the cup, rinsed it and scooped up a cupful of water to hand it to JoAnn quite nicely.

She drank from it.

Then he threw away the leftover water from the cup, wiped it with his handkerchief and scooped up another cupful and drank from it. She watched his tidiness. She was offended he'd wiped her contact away. She rejected him entirely.

She turned and began to walk back without waiting for him at all.

He caught up with her. "Don't hurry so. With my leg so badly hurt, I could get lost."

Coolly, she inquired, "No sense of direction?"

"None."

"The sun is there. That is east. We are to the south side of the sun."

He mentioned with sharing, "I don't believe I ever realized I could use the sun to guide me."

"What did you use?"

"A compass."

"You need to consider the sun. With the changes in the year, the sun changes. Pay attention."

She was discarding him. He knew that right away. He didn't know why.

He looked at her and she did not return his look. Her attention was on beyond. She didn't speak.

"I've offended you?"

She retorted, "Not at all. You are you."

Whatever he was, he'd sure as hell lost her. He said, "Could we walk a little slower? My leg—" That would catch her compassion.

"I've a phone call to make. See that tree ahead? That's even with the ranch house. Go thataway."

And she...just...strode on off! Leaving him there on the tableland all by himself! It was amazing.

He called, "It was your idea to walk, and I accompanied you. It is your commitment to see me back safely!" He was stern.

She hesitated. She walked slower. She was obviously considering her responsibility. She slowed more. She turned and put her hands on her hips. She asked, "How long are you going to milk that supposedly harmed leg?"

He was shocked. He looked at her in such amazement. "Do you think I was not harmed with the dead horse lying on my leg for over two days?"

"You've healed. You're milking this whole shebang. You bore me. Hustle up and let's get this over with."

Wiping his forehead with a pristine handkerchief, he said, "I must go slower. My leg—"

"—is in good condition. It only needs exercise. I asked your doctor. He thinks you're capable of using the leg without any cane. He especially asked about the cane I had mentioned."

Approaching her more slowly, he countered, "At the bottom of the stairs is a container of odd canes. I borrowed one." That was well said. He explained the cane without mentioning he didn't need one.

So she said it. "You don't need a cane."

He looked around. He gestured. "This is wild and woolly land. I needed some sort of protection...for you...out here."

It was courteous and he bowed his head just a trifle as he watched her.

She said, "Baloney." Then she turned and began to walk away—ahead of him, but at his pace. She did not speak to him. He mentioned things he observed which wasn't easy because the tableland was level and empty.

She did not reply in any way. She was really angry. She had better things to do with her time.

But then she began to remember what a good person her mother was and how her mother loved Mrs. Keeper. It was a nuisance. JoAnn didn't need this type of experience. She disliked a sly man who pretended to be more fragile than he was.

Then she considered his father who pretended to be fragile so that his wife paid close attention to him. And JoAnn considered the male population en masse. Men are strange. They *are* strange. But what else do women have to mate with?

With hostile endurance, she looked at Andrew. He was biting his lower lip as he watched along the way. He was in pain. His brow was wet. He wasn't faking it. She slowed down.

She stopped and sat down on the ground to empty a collection of dirt from her shoes. He watched her. She ignored him, but she'd given him a breather.

With her shoes carefully emptied, she carefully put them back on. She asked, "Are your shoes filled... you have boots?"

"Yeah."

"Good. That's smart on this land." She'd given him a compliment.

He said in a sharing manner, "I've worn boots since I came home from England."

"How long were you there?"

"Through my school years."

"Why did you want to go...there?"

"My parents."

"I wonder why they sent you...there."

"My daddy likes my mother's full attention." There. He'd said it out loud.

"Some parents are thataway. It's no problem. We have our own lives to live and can't change theirs."

Andrew looked at JoAnn in an entirely different way. In one day he'd gone from rejecting her to understanding she was smarter than he thought.

Four

It was after breakfast the next day. JoAnn dressed in a long-sleeved shirt with cotton trousers and boots. She went to the busy, distracted Mrs. Keeper and said, "I probably should just go on home. Andrew Parsons is beyond my lure. He treats me as if I am a child who is obstinately in another world from his. I agree."

Mrs. Keeper chided, "Darling, you can't abandon me now. I still have to find *some*one to help the poor man come along into current reality. You must stay just a while longer. It won't kill you to endure him. Your staying a while and distracting Andrew would help me tremendously."

Suspiciously, JoAnn asked, "Is this coercion?"

Mrs. Keeper put a sympathetic hand to her own

tousled hair as she replied, "Why…yes. I believe it could be called that. I need you."

Levelly, JoAnn retorted, "You said that you were looking for someone to take my place."

Shocked, Mrs. Keeper exclaimed, "Oh, I *am*, darling. I am searching for a woman who will jibe with Andrew. This just isn't at *all* simple. Be kind. Be patient. You can help this poor man." Then she tacked on: "Your mother loves you…too." She'd just barely remembered to add on that last word.

The almost forgotten last word indicated Mrs. Keeper remembered she also loved JoAnn who was precious. JoAnn very much doubted being precious or loved by Mrs. Keeper.

Disgruntled, aware she was being used, and her own mother was a part of the conspiracy, JoAnn advised, "Keep looking. You must find someone and *soon!*" She gave Mrs. Keeper a very hostile stare and squinted her eyes in a rather mean manner.

Mrs. Keeper sighed from her very toes and said, "I'm spending all my waking time…searching."

As JoAnn turned away, she warned, "Get to it." She was heartless.

It was time for JoAnn to find Andrew and communicate with him. Good gravy! This was not what she was raised to do. Her mother could not know exactly why the Keepers needed to keep this asinine guest. This Andrew Parsons didn't know beans!

Then she thought, hmmmm—maybe she could… change him. Maybe she could actually bring him up-to-date? Civilize him for the woman Mrs. Keeper would find for him? Yeah, she could do that. She didn't have anything else to entertain her.

Yesterday, he had actually talked about the Russian space station! That was certainly current. Maybe he wasn't as badly focused as Mrs. Keeper thought!

So, thinking her own way, JoAnn went in search of the boogeyman. He was the kind her daddy had warned her about long ago. He'd said if she kept on getting out of bed and exploring in the night when she was a child, she would find just such a person. Fathers tend to be hyper.

Andrew Parsons was not hyper. He was self-centered and obnoxious.

Since she didn't care about him one way or the other, and she wasn't at all afraid of him, she would simply entertain herself. She would pry things out of him and reject them all, slowly making him into a better man.

She found him in the garden. He was wearing a hat, a long-sleeved shirt tucked into khaki pants, and he was whistling as if expecting someone, something, to answer.

Andrew turned and saw JoAnn. He said, "Good morning."

Instead of responding to his greeting, she asked, "What are you whistling for?"

With undue patience, he mentioned, "My dog is missing."

She looked around. "He isn't around here. When did you realize he was gone?"

"Yesterday."

"And you're only looking for him now?"

"He can generally take care of himself...and me. But he has vanished."

That boggled her. A tad more strident, she repeated, "Only now, you're calling for him?"

"I looked for him yesterday when we walked."

"He was gone yesterday, but you didn't whistle then."

"I looked."

"And you could see if he was in the grasses or stubby growth?"

"You are implying that he was harmed or dead?"

She shrugged. "He didn't respond. Did he vanish? Did you send him somewhere? When did you last see him?"

Andrew found her irritating, but she was better than the silence he'd had to endure. He didn't say it had been several days since Buddy had asked to leave his room. Instead Andrew said, "It was the other morning."

JoAnn echoed with underlined snottiness, "The other morning. When have you looked for him? I haven't been aware of you watching for a dog or calling him."

"He'll turn up."

"If he isn't in some trap."

Andrew looked at her coldly. "A trap?"

"Ranchers have all sorts of traps for mice and rats and coyotes."

Andrew was indignant. "Why would anyone do that?"

"No rancher wants to support such creatures. The

animals proliferate, take up room, eat ranch animals' foods, or the animals themselves and are a nuisance.''

"So."

She shrugged. "They are controlled."

"Controlled." He tested the word.

"That means they are killed off but not entirely."

Andrew, the one who knew everything about a man in this country, retorted, "They are killed? That seems rather rude."

"It's logical. The ranches can't allow too many creatures to eat in live off the land around them. Your dog could be in some coyote trap."

He instantly looked around, stretching up to see farther. "Where are the traps?"

She indicated the area. "Along the animal trails."

"Where are those?"

"You don't know about animal trails?"

"I've never seen any."

"And you are a man of the past? When do you think snaring animals began?"

"I have never snared an animal. It is ruthless and cruel."

"So you've heard of it?"

"On occasion."

"But you didn't find out what it was."

He looked at her stony face with eyes that were equally stony. He disliked her.

She waited.

He made no reply. He moved away. He whistled. There was no reply. He put his two fingers into his mouth and whistled shrilly. He knew it was impressive. That'd break her damned eardrums.

She didn't even flinch.

They both looked and listened. Nothing responded. Some birds flew over but they were flying high and might have been on their way anyway. Nothing came. Nothing was curious. All was quiet.

Birds sang. TEXAS birds always sing. The scissortails flew. They are odd birds with tails crossed like open scissors.

There were mockingbirds who could mock any of the other birds. One—or maybe more than one—had sleepily echoed the Swiss cuckoo clock JoAnn's mother had. But the bird was dumb. It didn't quit at twelve sounds at midnight. It just went on a little beyond that. Then trilled a few other birds' comments before it went back to sleep.

JoAnn lifted her face. She wore a wide brimmed cowboy hat to shade her from the sun. It was just right. Closing her eyes, she breathed the TEXAS air and was filled with the fragrance.

Andrew realized she was a very well-made female. How could he shut her up and just enjoy her body? He considered her. Then he managed to look away when she turned her head.

He whistled again.

She mentioned, "Obviously, your dog cannot hear you since he has not responded to your whistle from this point. I would suggest you move to another area."

That was irritatingly logical. The suggestion offended Andrew. She thought *he* should move? The dog should come to him! He looked at her with about the same expression he gave spinach. He retorted as if he'd known what she'd volunteered, "Of course."

They walked in silence. They looked for the dog. After a while, she commented on the outdoors. She said, "I love coming here. Being in a town isn't what I want."

"You're an outdoor girl?"

"—woman."

He licked his lips to hide his humor about this harridan. He courteously echoed, "—woman."

"I like it both ways," she told him. She lifted her chin and looked around. She didn't miss a thing. She saw no dog tracks nor did she see a dog. She told him, "Whistle again." And she put her fingers in her ears.

He rather liked it that she had to protect her ears from his whistle. He took a deep breath and gave the Come Here *now* whistle.

The dog did not appear.

She said, "He's dead or he's run off after some bitch."

Andrew's eyes slid over and he looked down her body. He could understand a brief encounter with a female. He inquired, "Does your mother know you use that word so carelessly?"

"No. I protect her ears' fragile knowledge."

He said with snide courtesy, "How kind."

She allowed that to slide on off. She didn't give two hoots what he thought. She mentioned kindly, "Since I know the territory, I would suggest you try that area—" she pointed to the west, northwest "—for your—"

"Why, there?"

"If you will allow me, I shall finish my sentence— dog, because there are many kinds of small, easily caught animals in that particular area. Notice that the ground is rather a tilted soup plate. The trees are closer. It is warm in winter and cool in summer. And herds avoid the crush of the trees."

"The shade?" He touched on that sounding kindly.

"The prickly cactus."

"*Ahhhh.*"

"Yes."

So she knew the territory. Andrew slid his eyes over to her in such a way that he could avoid looking at her if she was watching him. She was ignoring him. Now that was interesting to know. She didn't like him. So why did she seek him out? Probably for the very reason he tolerated her? There wasn't anyone else that she could talk with?

Boredom is worldwide. The solutions are mostly what had happened to the two of them. JoAnn and Andrew. They were together, speaking reasonably and searching for a dog. Together. Together because it was easier than being alone.

Andrew had learned about being alone early in his life. And he realized he was being as aloof to this female as he'd had to tolerate and survive in England. He could be kinder.

He asked, "Are you kin to the Keepers?"

She replied simply, "Friends."

She did not elaborate. So he inquired, "How...did the friendship start and between who?"

"School. My mother and Mrs. Keeper."

Chatty, wasn't she? He sought questions. He'd never interviewed or begun any conversation with anyone, at anytime. He tried to think how to open her head up so that she would talk.

He asked, "Your mother was a classmate of Mrs. Keeper?"

"Yes."

What a reply! "What school?"

"You wouldn't know it. It's a woman's school over in the south. Exclusive."

He said briefly, "Money."

"Not necessarily. The board is of women who went there. They are very open. There are scholarships. The students are well trained, and the teas were delightful."

"We had teas in England. They were rigid."

"You only went to school there?" And before he could reply, she asked, "Why?"

"My daddy was jealous of me. He wanted my mother's full attention."

"*Awww.*"

Somehow he didn't want her sympathy so he said, "I got along okay." There was a blatant understatement if he'd ever heard one.

Their intrusion into the soup plate area was interesting. Andrew whistled and just that shut up everything. But the dog, Buddy, did not respond. They continued their search.

They were careful. With the silencing of the go-phers and birds and coyotes and the hostile scolding of the squirrels, there were a lot of muted and hushed rustles.

There were snakes. Andrew watched where he put his feet. JoAnn got a little hyper. Andrew did not whisper. He wanted his dog to hear him. He said to JoAnn, "Watch where you step."

She let him go first. He had on shoes. She had on boots. She figured if he went first, she would see any movement after he'd passed. She watched.

Andrew watched the ground also but he mostly looked around, and he called to his dog. There were rustles but no replying barks.

They looked carefully, but Buddy was not there.

They went out of the tree-covered, cactus-covered soup plate and stood quietly on the other side of the nature dish. It had been a try.

They looked beyond and saw the different, used area of grass and mostly Keeper-planted old oak trees with hackberry trees along and around. They were gnarled and interesting. Along the fence lines, under the mesquites, there were sparse growths of weeds.

JoAnn looked over at the useless Andrew who waited for someone to talk to him or to ask him ques-tions or to expound on his long, wasted life. How could he be brought up to current?

Why did he avoid realizing his time was now and that was all he had?

He would lie in his coffin and his spirit would jab-ber away…too late, unheard? Probably even if he could be heard, he had nothing of real interest to say. How demeaning. How sad.

JoAnn asked, "Shall we search farther or go back to the house?"

"Let's see if there's a reason for that drop-off over yonder."

She looked across the plain to where he pointed. "You believe the Keepers pitch unwanted guests off there?"

He considered her and decided he wouldn't actually pitch her. There was no one else who chatted with him. So he replied to the pitching, "Perhaps."

She couldn't stop a rumbling of humor. "I'll stand back a way, but I'll walk over with you so that you can see."

He cautioned, "You're not to trip me or push me off, do you understand? I would come back and haunt you with all the boring, discarded tales I've gathered."

She rejected that, "I think you're too heavy for me to tilt over the edge."

"So you've already considered that!"

She replied, "A mind considers all sorts of things."

He considered her. "You'd be light and easy to pitch over the edge."

She faked high tension and stuttered anxiously through the words, "Don't pitch me over the edge. Promise!"

"Well, darn. You spoil any guy's pleasures." He was so amused.

She laughed.

"You *trust* me?"

She retorted, "Any man who spends all this time trying to locate a lost dog, *must* have some sterling character in him."

"You are misled."

"You're a rake?"

They were already walking across the flatland to the drop. He replied, "I've been discarded by just about everyone I know."

That caught her attention. He was not kidding. He was serious. She asked, "How'd you manage that?"

"Actually, I'm not at all sure. I suspect even my dog has abandoned me. He asked to be let out of the room, and I did that. He left."

"Why would he leave you?"

"I forgot to feed him supper. I was so furious that I wasn't served, that I just forgot the dog. He was hungry."

"When did you realize you hadn't fed him?"

"After he left, he didn't return. I saw that I hadn't opened any of his food. It was I who was at fault."

"He'll forgive you."

"If he's alive."

"You think he could have died of hunger?"

"I'm not sure."

"Well, I think the crew would have fed a hungry dog if they'd come across one. They are very compassionate to any dog or person who is hungry. You don't have to worry. You've been here how many days?"

"I think it's about five. I can't keep track well enough. I just came from the hospital." He added that rather quickly. Actually, he'd been there a day short of two weeks.

JoAnn watched him and said nicely, "You're walking very well. Are you all right?"

He said slowly, "I may have to sit down and rest."

"We'll find a place."

He smiled with gentleness, but his mind blinked its eyes slowly and there was a snorted laugh inside his head.

They actually strolled to the other side of that flatland and climbed the bank the Keepers had built to keep the dirt from washing away into the canyon. Silently, they stood to look down into the drop that was before them. It was there. It was not controlled land. It was wild and beautiful like looking down on something God just made.

They looked at what was before them and felt as if they were the first to ever even see it. But they knew from the plowed field behind them that it was no surprise to anyone who lived there.

They didn't even bother to exclaim or comment. There it all was. Silently, they looked and filled their souls.

There was an outjut of rock on the beginning, down-sloping of the land. Andrew went over to it and considered it. The slope was not dangerous at first and there were other outcroppings that could delay a fall.

He tested the jutted rock and it seemed entirely solid. He sat on it rather heavily and bounced several times. It did not move. He said to JoAnn, "Try it."

"You sit there. I'll sit on the ground." It was too intimate to sit so close.

He waited until she was settled about ten feet away from him. Then he sat easily on the outcropping.

The scene before them was a gift. It was so beautiful. It was so peaceful. It was awesome.

After some time, she inquired, "Was this made just for us?"

"Probably."

"Why...probably."

So he was truthful. "I have come to a crossroad in my life. I was bitter. This makes me feel as if the world may not have been made just for my own interest."

"Well, damn! I thought all the time it was made for *me!*"

Andrew laughed. He laughed softly, but then he found he was too amused and he couldn't swallow all those sounds, so he laughed out loud...and the echoes of his laughter bounced joyfully around in the hollows and against the walls before them.

She was so charmed and so amused and delighted that her own laughter mixed in with his.

They did not touch. They exchanged glances now and again. But they were separate.

They settled down, relaxed and amused. And they just looked at what was around them. They didn't speak. They both knew why they'd laughed. It was in separate ways. His was astonishment that he was there and still alive.

JoAnn laughed because it echoed so well. Two different reasons.

His was joy of a kind of surprise.

She laughed to hear the echoes. The intertwined echoes of shared laughter.

Nothing fell. No rocks slid with the vibrations of their laughter. Other people had called and shouted and laughed before them.

They had no water. They hadn't planned to be out that long. But they each found a small smooth rock to put in their different mouths to suck on them It made their saliva trickle into their dry mouths.

They walked back to the house, which was closer from the tableland rift than the eastern area had been when they were searching for the dog.

She asked, "How'd you know to come this way back to the house?"

"My compass."

"I shall get one."

"I have several. You may have one of mine."

"Why…thank you."

"I have enjoyed our companionship."

That sounded very like a farewell. She considered how she should reply. She finally said, "This has been a pleasant day."

"For me, too."

As they came to a west side approach to the house, they could see it through the trees. There was a spring there, and they stopped and drank from it. What all drank there? Well, the creatures wouldn't have hepatitis or typhoid fever. The way it overflowed into the stream, it was pure.

And a bird flew over to deny that little supposition.

Andrew lifted his curled fingers up as if he held the handle of a gun and said, "Pow."

She laughed. Boys played cowboy all their young lives. Here was another.

He blew off his invisible smoking gun and said, "Do you see him?"

"The bird?"

"Yes."

She looked up and around. It was gone. She said, "Poor bird. You ought not shoot those who only are indiscreet." She licked her smile to cover it.

"It teaches them not to do it again."

"What a stickler!"

"Yeah."

She said thoughtfully, "You are not of the live-and-let-live believers."

"No."

"It's good to know that about you."

He inquired, "So that you will respect me?"

"So that I will avoid you."

"Why would you...avoid me?"

Her voice was oddly gentle. "I don't agree with you. You will not be changed. You are too long in the tooth to correct yourself and your ideas."

In assimilating all that, Andrew tilted his head and squinched his eyes as he tasted the words, "Too long in the tooth to...correct...myself. That means you don't believe I can change."

"More than likely."

"You are a woman who thinks without any guidance."

"Correct."

He looked at her. "So I have for once been…correct?"

"Several times. But they aren't important. The important ones are the ones you won't change."

"Like—"

"Pretending to kill the bird. The only reason you pretended is that you didn't have a gun with you."

He slid his hand into his pocket and pulled out a small pistol. It would have to be close, but it was lethal.

She lowered her head in respect and commented, "By the time you got it out, the bird would have been gone."

He said, "Let's test that comment." He put the gun back in his pant pocket.

She felt around on herself, which *fascinated* him and, after feeling her pockets, she came up with a quarter. She flipped it up, and he shot it before it began to fall.

She said, "You're practiced."

"Anyone who travels alone must be prepared in this day and time."

She corrected, "In *any* day or time."

"Yes."

"So you believe this is a dangerous time and you carry a gun?"

"Yes."

"You scare me a little."

"You scare me a hell of a lot."

And she was baffled. "Why?"

"You could ruin me."

"I don't know much, at all, about you. How could I ruin you?"

"By luring me into your trap."

She laughed in whoops. She laughed until she had to stop and lean one hand against a tree. The tree was what told her she was nearer the house. She assimilated that and continued to laugh. She found a handkerchief and blotted her eyes and discreetly blew her nose. She said, "You're hilarious."

"You're fantastic."

"Come on, Andrew, you could barely tolerate me until just now. You must be a needy man."

"No."

"You have women lined up?"

"No."

"You're out of your mind. If you really believe any of what you've just said, you aren't working with a full deck."

He was silent.

"No reply?"

"You wouldn't believe me."

She considered him. She said, "You're right. I wouldn't." And she walked on back toward the house...and he kept up.

So actually, that day, Andrew had walked about as far as the doctors and Mrs. Keeper had advised.

The fact that no one saw them speak was no surprise. Andrew was a nerd to everyone else in the area. If a good woman like JoAnn couldn't speak with him, it was no surprise to anyone else. Neither could they get Andrew to talk with them.

It was rather remarkable that no one came to JoAnn's room before dinner. She stripped and showered. Having dried herself with a large towel, she went to her bed and piled the pillows at the head of it.

Her beautifully made female body naked, she got into bed, pulled up the sheet and a small blanket, put earphones on her head and turned on the news.

JoAnn's stomach growled. Being a guest was a chore, but she'd always had snacks in her room. She opened the drawer of the bed table and pulled out a variety of cookies and fruit. She had a glass of water on the glass top of the bed table.

She watched the news. She didn't want to think or give any replies to anyone. Especially not to him. To the man with whom she'd walked. She not only didn't believe his words, but she also thought he was a middle-aged snot. He could hardly tolerate her before he'd changed at the end of that very day.

She figured he was a needy man, and he thought she'd be honored. Yeah. Sure.

Five

To go to dinner, Andrew Parsons bathed, quite carefully shaved and dressed with attention. He could use a haircut. Well, he would be okay for now. He'd see to the haircut tomorrow. He smiled at the mirror. He was pleased with his image.

JoAnn was about what he wanted. A little too independent, but available. And adjusted to— Actually, she had made *him* adjust. No, tolerate. She was firm and didn't give one inch! She had forced him to be civil. Hmmm. He'd thought *he* was the one in charge. He'd have to consider her more closely.

Close? He smiled into the mirror as he considered being…close…to her.

Carrying the unneeded cane with some élan, he walked down to the first floor where the dinners were held. There was a meeting room where they all gathered. It was attractive. They were offered quite small glasses of wine or fruit juice.

Andrew entered as would any known person. And Mrs. Keeper was kind enough to see him and gather people around him. He had a glass of wine.

Before then, he'd never realized how well Mrs. Keeper handled guests. She was firm that people talk to each other. She never loosened the social rope to allow them to drift away or to take over the conversations entirely. She was steel!

Mrs. Keeper was steel? Andrew was shocked. He observed the fragile—lady, for she was one. She was relentless. She guided the conversations. She knew what they each knew, and she pulled it out of them with such gentle tact that he was shivered. She was a steel woman, attractive and unbending but gently so.

Mrs. Keeper's manners were perfect. She appeared to be kind, gentle and a lady. However— If one observed and listened, everything went her way. She was courteously, gently relentless.

The really appalling part was what she did was right! That was demeaning.

Having assimilated the real facts about Mrs. Keeper, Andrew then glanced around again to see if JoAnn had yet arrived. She was not there. He smiled a bit in anticipation. He was eager to see her again.

Then...*then*...Mrs. Keeper said, "Shall we?" And she took the arm of the male who would be seated to her right, and they went into the dining room. The arm she accepted was not Andrew's.

He tagged along rather like a bit of wood caught in the current. Hmmm. He was not a bit of wood.

A footman found his place for him and indicated the chair in kind, smiling attention.

Andrew frowned. He was lost in the middle of the table. He looked to see where JoAnn would be. But it wasn't near to him. Damn.

He watched to see if the laggard got there in time or would she be late? The Keepers didn't encourage lateness.

The chairs were all filled? Where would she sit? He would offer his chair. She would be charmed by his gesture.

When JoAnn didn't appear, Andrew became concerned. He stretched up in order to see if she was there.

JoAnn.

It had taken him a while to realize she was special. She had been around like a flea in his shirt. Now the agitation was in his pants.

She did not arrive. Where was she? He could hardly get up and go see. He stopped one of the servers and said, "Miss Murray, the redhead? She isn't here."

And the server said, "I'll check."

Andrew remembered to say, "Thank you."

It was odd that he paid no attention to the people on either side of him. He did not assimilate what all they ate or what they said or disagreed about. Andrew had been picky and pushed things aside and ignored them. This time, he ate. It was probably because of the long walk. He was hungry.

If he was hungry, why wasn't JoAnn there? She'd

walked as far. Had she fainted in the shower? He signaled the server he'd spoken with.

That person came to Andrew and said, "Yes, Sir?" as he looked at Andrew's depleted plate.

"Miss Murray..."

"Someone has gone to her room. One of the women. She has a key. If there's no reply, she will enter the room. We are careful of our guests."

"Thank you."

"As soon as we know about her, we'll tell you."

"I appreciate that."

So one of the women went down the hall and tapped on JoAnn Murray's door as she listened carefully.

From inside the room came, "Who is it?"

"It's I, Ginny. Mr. Parsons was concerned about you not being at the table."

JoAnn said through the door, "I've decided to skip supper."

The woman asked, "Is there anything I can bring to you?"

"Thanks, but no."

The woman said, "Sleep well."

JoAnn replied, "I shall."

And that was the sum of it all. JoAnn Murray was going to sleep. So the woman went back and told the server what had been said to her through the door, and he went to Andrew and said, "Miss Murray is going to sleep."

While that shocked Andrew, he realized they'd walked too far—for JoAnn. She was exhausted. He should have paid more attention. He ate his second plateful more slowly. He replied with courtesy to the openings given him. He started no conversation nor did he ask any questions of his own. He didn't know to do that. He only knew he was primary.

Andrew felt he'd done his share of table talk in replying. When he could, he excused himself from the table and walked out of the room. He went to JoAnn's door and tapped quietly so that if she was asleep, she would not waken, but if she was awake, she'd come to her door.

She did not come to the door nor did she open it. She heard the quiet tap and surmised it was Andrew. She did not want to talk to him...at all. She was fed up with the struggle each time of making him pliant. She'd done her share. *Any*thing would slide him back into being a snot. She wanted nothing more to do with him.

Why not?

She sighed with endurance at her other half and retorted in her brain, "He's a winky-dink. He loves himself. He isn't a part of the general population. He feels he is unique. He is not unique at *all*, he is a bore."

Her other self considered that reply and thoughtfully agreed it was probably so.

So her two other parts, which enjoyed debate, settled down and watched TV while the sound was in her earphones. Gradually, she yawned. Then she drank some water. And finally she blinked off the TV, removed the earphones and settled down to sleep.

She dreamed. In her dream, Andrew was missing.

Not his dog but *he* was missing. He'd gone to walk and gotten lost. He had had the compass, and he knew how to read it. He'd lost it when he'd fallen. Why had he fallen? He'd been looking back to see if she followed him.

Why in this *world* would she be out—following him?

Uhhhhhhhh…curiosity? She wanted to know if he could walk again after that dead horse had been lying on his leg for over some fifty hours.

Her nonunsell thought, that was some time ago. He was just about completely recovered.

Yeah. Why the cane?

That was an asinine retort from her alter ego. It agreed with her. So she flopped over to go back to sleep. She didn't sleep. She lay and her eyelids opened. There was nothing interesting to look at. She could not again close her eyes. She ground her teeth.

Then she pried herself up, put on the earphones and turned the TV back on. There was a show on with some nighthawk who thought anything he said was clever. It was odd. Why did all those people laugh? That was baffling until she remembered the audience was given directions via printed cardboards.

She found a movie that was almost finished. It was extremely emotional and tense! JoAnn had no idea at *all* what was happening. That the people were horrifically upset was obvious but—

And some sort of flying something with a dark, wide, flapping cape came down and swooped the heroine away!

The heroine struggled and screamed at some

height. That was a stupid thing to do in those circumstances. So the woman fell from the sky and screamed even worse.

Such stupid conduct irritated the liver out of JoAnn and she turned off the TV. She lay in a lump. She was irritated. She wanted to go home.

Now, how was she going to manage that? She had been sent by her mother to help her mother's dear friend straighten out a man who didn't know about the real world. JoAnn did not want to have anything more to do with the blob who was the guest in question.

Although she rattled her brain, JoAnn could not find any other friend or semifriend who would come and help with the creature who was Andrew Parsons.

He was not only an irritating man, he was obsolete. Who wanted to deal with a man who felt like time was from over two *hundred* years ago when this country was just getting organized?

In San Antonio, the Alamo fell to the Mexicans in 1836.

Think of that. It was less than two hundred years ago. They had no trucks, no tanks. They rode horses and had guns that they had to reload with every time they'd been fired. All that was not even two hundred years ago!

They just had buggies, wagons, horses and shank's mare. That meant walking. If you had no horse, you walked.

In that time, there were no cars, no trains even. Not an airplane in sight of mind. Well, they'd had big kites some long, long time before. Thousands of years. A kite so big that a reckless man could ride one of the giants up in the air and look at what all might be coming their way.

And they used kites to figure the length of an intruding tunnel that would go under the wall of the castle they were accosting. JoAnn was glad she hadn't lived then, but her time was now.

Andrew was a man of a long-ago time.

Actually, was he that basic? He certainly liked his comfort and his food. He didn't know any of the sidelines of what all went on two hundred years ago. It was as if he wore horse blinders and saw only what he wanted to see. That was not uncommon.

But he was not genuine. He wasn't even a throwback. He was lazy…well, retiring. A loner. His parents ought to do something about him.

And she thought of his parents who sent him all that way to school in England just so that his father did not need to compete with his son.

—or was it vice versa?

Now, that was an interesting thing to understand. He had sisters. One was living with one of the flyers on the Keeper place. Andrew thought his sister, Lu, was still staying at the hospice.

He wasn't too bright.

He probably needed help. JoAnn sighed.

However—

He had spoken with knowledge about the Russian space station. Hmmm. And she wondered why he played the throwback. Why was he…hiding in time? She spent restless time thinking of that, as she moved

in her bed and rustled the sheet and plumped up her
pillow.

So the next day, JoAnn chose to have breakfast in
bed. She was starving and ate every bit. She showered. Then she made her own bed. It was a tumbled
mess, and she wasn't going to have any maid gossip
about her restlessness.

Dressed in a shirt and trousers and wearing riding
boots, she searched for Mrs. Keeper. Oddly, JoAnn
never managed contact. That irritated JoAnn somewhat but she felt she'd done her best to communicate.

So, freed of obligations, JoAnn searched for a place
and found a small, second floor sunroom with a few
chairs. She checked out the wall of books, selected
one, sat in a chair with her back to the window, put
her feet on the other chair and opened the book to
read.

—and Andrew found her.

He'd had one heck of a time searching her out. Her
room was neat and empty. She hadn't shared breakfast with the rest of the group. It never even *once*
occurred to Andrew that she was avoiding him.

Why else would she be in such an isolated place
as that very small sunroom?

Andrew said cheerfully, "So you're reading."

A brilliant approach.

She slowly turned her head while her eyes stayed
on the page. Then she looked up at him sober-faced.
She asked, "Some problem?"

"I was concerned when you didn't come for supper
last night. Obviously, you were tired from our walk."

She demurred, "I wasn't hungry."

His lips parted and he became serious. "How could you not have been hungry? We were out for quite a while. Are you ill?"

"Not at all." She went back to her book.

He sat down and looked around.

She didn't look up or speak.

Andrew said, "This is charming."

She slowly put her finger on the page and gradually looked up. Then she asked, "What?"

"This place. I didn't know it was here. I find it charming."

She considered him as one does some odd, rather distasteful thing in a zoo. As her eyes dropped, she said, "Ummm." She went back to her reading.

Having spent so much time in England with people who were different, he wasn't put off. He looked at the books and finally chose one with some satisfaction. He sat down by a low table away from her and opened the book.

He felt very relaxed and sharing to be reading, with her there and also reading.

She had abandoned him. Discarded him. Forgotten him. He was like a fly caught on flypaper. She'd seen some once at her grandmother's house. Too many people went in and out of a porch door and her grandmother got fed up with flies coming in also.

So grandmother had hung up the flypaper and the flies were ignorant enough to think anything that smelled that nice must be tasty. The new flies, entering, obviously figured the cries of warning from the captured flies were only selfishness since they were eating the yummy smelling stuff on the paper.

There JoAnn was, hiding on a "paper" and here he was, another fly, caught.

How would she release herself from this flytrap? She could get up and excuse herself. She did that.

He rose as he asked, "Where are we going?"

She could say she wasn't feeling well and would go lie down. How dull.

But if she did say she wasn't feeling well, he would take her elbow and insist that he take her over to the medical center.

That place was on the other side of the ranch. It was a separate two story house with a large fenced area that was quartered nicely.

The medics took care of anything that wasn't feeling up to par. They took care of the staff and houseguests and whatever ailed.

But the medical crew mostly saw animals who had eaten something stupid, or got tangled up in something wicked, or had been in a fight of some kind, that sort of thing.

Some years back while visiting the Keepers with her mother, JoAnn had gone there with a sprained wrist. She'd had to wait while the medic looked at a barbwire ripped horse.

In TEXAS, it was said as "bobed" wire? That is a TEXAS questioning, do-you-understand statement.

Even then, JoAnn could understand the horse came first, and she helped one-handed to comfort the horse. The medics had bragged about her help. They didn't mention she'd been in their way.

But JoAnn didn't want to be dragged to the medical clinic so she would have to cope with Andrew Parsons. Why couldn't Mrs. Keeper find someone else for this Parsons person? Life was a drag. It made a thinker wonder, Why are we scheduled to cope with so many whatevers before we fade away and die?

So she considered Andrew next to her in that hidden place she'd found—and so had he. She asked, "Why do we live on this planet and cope?"

He lifted his eyes from his book, quite interested. He inquired, "Cope?"

She circled a hand as she said, "With the other people and other things and weather and food and what all."

Andrew guessed, "It's…stimulating?"

JoAnn denied that, "Not especially."

So Andrew put down his book and considered her question and attitude. He said, "Life would be boring if it wasn't for the horizon, the weather, eating, seeing someone who was attractive and wanting her."

"There *has* to be something more to living than the—horizon—the weather and eating."

He smiled. "You skipped seeing someone who was attractive."

She examined all that in her mind and then said, "So…you're just here, in this place, in order to find someone who attracts you?"

He smiled at her and his eyes twinkled. "It changes a man's life and outlook and gives him something to plan for."

That frightened JoAnn's stomach. She didn't want him considering her. And God help whoever if some other woman had attracted him in the meantime and JoAnn hadn't been told.

Then she considered, if Andrew had seen someone who attracted him last night, he wouldn't be up there in that tiny, secret room...with her. Was he saying he was attracted to—JoAnn Murray? Surely Fate was smarter than that.

Of course, Mrs. Keeper was more intelligent than to consider throwing Andrew and her together until he was smitten with JoAnn and willing.

Her eyes moved over and she considered his body. He was in good shape. His body was masculine. No question. He walked carefully, like a man who expects to find a surprise.

She inquired, "In England, were the other boys rough with you?"

"Not at all. They ignored me. They had their own cliques and didn't need me at all. They didn't shun me, they just never noted that I was also there."

And with his words, Andrew understood he'd forgiven them all. How strange to realize that. The realization made him want to go back for that year's reunion and look at them all again, with clear, seeing eyes.

He said, "I may go back for the year's gathering over yonder in Britain. Here, it's like our country's Homecoming Week. The place is packed." But he again saw an isolated one in the middle of all that and recognized himself. He'd been so lonely.

JoAnn said, "At our school over in the southern states, it is a shrill, laughing round of endless exclamations."

He smiled. "Anybody would feel a lift at just seeing you."

Those words were so kind and different, that her stomach was scared. She said, "I have to make a call. Will you excuse me?"

"I'll go with you and be sure the Keepers don't have coin telephones."

Her mouth parted in shock, then she laughed. "They encourage long-distance calls. They like hearing from and about other people."

"They are very kind."

He really surprised JoAnn. Andrew had said that the Keepers were—kind. He understood what good hosts they were. His thinking was changing? He was becoming…human? He might be easier to palm off on to some other woman with less of a conscience twinge. She asked, "Do you like blondes or brunettes?"

He looked at her red hair. "I like something a bit different. I like someone who is unique." And he was amused by his subtlety. His eyes danced and he licked his smile to quiet it.

But he scared the spit out of JoAnn. She tilted her head and said, "I'll look for women for you. As you know, I've been appointed to find you someone who would interest you."

"*You*… interest me."

"I'm not available."

He became quite solemn. "Who is he?"

"That isn't important at this time. We need to know what sort of woman is interesting to you." So.

She'd spilled the plot. He would now know that she was one of those involved in finding him a wife.

He said with élan, "I don't know of any reason to look any farther. You delight me."

"Balderdash! You can hardly endure being around me!"

He was open. "That was then. I've come to know you. I find you...charming."

"Baloney. You're bored out of your gourd. Anyone will do."

"Well, don't discard being female." He grinned with great charm.

She watched him with squinted eyes for a short, silent time and then she said, "You must be desperate."

He watched her cautiously with intensely riveted interest. "—for you."

Her body lax, JoAnn shook her head from side to side in exasperation. She said, "Let's back up to just yesterday when you wanted to drop me in a hole to get rid of me, and stomp dirt in on top of me. You couldn't change in this short a time."

He grinned slightly, and his eyes danced with her words. He said in a considering way, "I suppose you wouldn't know of all the women who tag along trying for my attention. They are mostly as good-looking as you—don't protest, just accept that you are a gem.

"But so are most women." He admitted that. "I just don't long to be the interest of a woman who only wants a—thrill." He lifted his hand as he considered his words intently. "A woman who wants—" he sought the word "—a—" he shook his head and his face was intense as he stumbled for the word "—a thrill that is brief. Something to mark a check in her clothes closet? A winner of a time." He looked at JoAnn.

She nodded. "Some women do that. They take after men. Probably some man used them thataway, and the women are finding revenge of a kind?"

He said earnestly serious, "I'm not trying to...use you."

She discarded his reply and explained, "You need a wife."

So he grinned and replied, "Okay."

And that went over her head as she said earnestly, "Mrs. Keeper is supposed to've found one for you. The woman is to come here so that you can look at her and agree, or reject her with some discretion so that she won't be devastated."

"That is considerate. I don't need to see another woman. I've seen you. You are willing to bend, you are interested in the land and in the creatures we've seen." He was earnest. "You walk along and see things as you look around. You're a jewel."

"I'm not interested in getting married or being the 'friend' of someone at this time."

"We'll take it easy."

"There are women who are coming here for you to see. Promise you will be courteous and kind to them."

"I would be."

"You were about as rude as any person I've ever known. I had no desire for you nor do I want to see if you can be courteous until you have your way."

He was shocked. "Have I been rude?"

"You know damned good and well you've been a snot!"

"Wow! As bad as that?" He looked at her with interest.

Carefully, she enunciated, "I was being subtle and courteous."

"If my mother heard that report, she would have gone into a decline."

JoAnn shook her head. "I don't spill the beans. But I don't want anything to do with you. Mrs. Keeper asked me here to help you find a wife. I have asked her for release. She has said I may leave—"

He gasped and looked dismayed.

"—as soon as she finds someone to replace me. I thought I'd been asked to come and just run you off. I'm especially good at that. Then I found she wants to find you a wife. God only knows who that would be."

"Not you?"

"Absolutely not."

"Oh."

"Tell me what sort of woman you might cotton to. Give me a physical idea. Tall or short—that sort of thing." She found a pad and pencil. The Keepers would have something like that everywhere in a house...car...tractor? Whatever.

Andrew looked soberly at JoAnn and said very carefully, "I like redheads."

She wrote that down and asked, "Age?"

"How old are you?"

She looked up and inquired, "Do gentlemen ask that?"

"I was just getting an idea of the age area."

"I'm too old to marry. I'm thirty."

"Well, I'm older than you and I wouldn't want to have to deal with a youngster who doesn't have any idea how she's supposed to act or what she's supposed to do with a husband, a house or kids."

"So you want children." It was a statement. And she wrote that down.

"Not with a child bride. It'd be like suffering through a double dose of kids."

She could understand that. So she squinted her eyes and said, "Actually, someone closer in age should be better. How old would you say she should be?"

"Oh, about...thirty?"

She considered and advised him, "You're not going to get many—untried—women at that age."

"How many men have you...experienced?"

"We're not talking about me. We're talking about reality."

Six

Actually, it was Mina Keeper who racked her brain and invited a niece to come to meet Andrew. Through the phone line, she told her niece, Cynthia, "Darling, the situation here is a very shaky thing, and you must be careful."

Through the phone and in Mina's ear, Cynthia said, "Fascinating. When should I arrive?"

"Tomorrow?"

"Uhhhh…I'll…have to…adjust a few things. But I love you, and I'll be there."

In a deadly voice, Mina said, "I am counting on you. You will use your skills and be astonishing to JoAnn? She believes she does not care for Andrew."

"I'll rock her!" Cynthia laughed, then she added, "You're just lucky I love you because—" she sighed into the mouthpiece with excellent drama "—I'll have to cancel a time with Peter."

In an open threat, Mina enunciated, "Do not bring him along."

"I won't! I won't! Do you think I'm nuts? I've *seen* JoAnn! Look for me at eight—"

Mina corrected relentlessly, "Tomorrow—at—*ten*. Don't get pushy."

So Cynthia arrived at the Keeper place on the TEXAS Tablelands at ten-of-five. How like her to tilt the time just a tad to show independence. She was cheerful, amused and gorgeous. She came into the house and called, "I'm *here!*"

And anybody within Cynthia's rather awesome range of voice, came a-running...to crowd those already gathered around the new guest. Cynthia accepted that as right.

Mina called out, but she wasn't the first to hug Cynthia. She pulled one of the hands off her niece and scolded, "You're *supposed* to be taking care of the Western herd out yonder." She pointed in that direction.

He grinned and said, "I am." Then he hollered, "Line up! Don't make a maelstrom outta this here greetings."

Mina found her mind tasting that. Maelstrom? How'd Rusty ever stumble onto a word like...maelstrom? Then Mina said out loud to her niece, "Welcome to the Keepers. We'll discuss, quite seriously, whether we'll let you leave."

How flattering.

Mina hugged Cynthia and then stood by her as the others pushed to greet their guest. More greeters poured into the hall as others were moved aside. They were all delighted to see Cynthia, and each thought he/she was the one Cynthia loved the most. There were the delighted eyes of females, and the zonked eyes of the males.

And she met Andrew.

Where had he come from? Well, in the line, he was just after JoAnn whose eyes were shocked by who was behind her. She stood and stared at Andrew's greeting of Cynthia like some flawed statue that had been misplaced.

Andrew shook Cynthia's hand and he said kindly, "They've been wild, waiting for you to get here. The whole, entire place!"

Cynthia looked at the calm, unagitated male before her as something entirely unheard of, at all. She smiled her flipping-male smile and said, "Well, hello."

"Everybody here is excited you got here. I can see why." Then Andrew stepped aside and took hold of the hand the white-faced, stunned JoAnn owned. He looked at her. Then he asked directly, "You okay?"

And she managed to mutter, "Yeah."

But inside her head was a buzz of shock that was the repetitive, whipping sounds of a mindlessly astonished: "He wasn't zonked!"

Then JoAnn frowned. How come, he—wasn't? And she stared at him as if he might melt like sunburned chocolate.

Andrew did not melt. He smiled at the enthusiastic

greetings to Mrs. Keeper's niece. He knew Cynthia
was a friend of his love. She was there for JoAnn?
That was nice.

Andrew thought JoAnn looked a little odd. He
asked her again, "You okay?"

Still in shock, she stared at Andrew. He could look
at something *else* besides Cynthia? What was the matter with him? And she squinted her eyes earnestly to
see if he was real and honest.

But what honest man could drag his eyes away
from Cynthia? Why could Andrew just look not at
Cynthia but at *her* so earnestly and ask, "Honey, are
you all right?"

She nodded in an undisciplined manner.

He stood by JoAnn and put his supportive arm
around her wilted form. She needed the support. All
she could think of was that Andrew had survived
meeting…Cynthia. How incredible.

And she figured it out. He was immune because he
thought of no one but—himself.

Uhhhh… If that was true, why was he so concerned
about—her? He was holding her scared, stupid body
and keeping her from slithering down to the floor in
a puddle. *Andrew* had survived meeting *Cynthia!*

JoAnn was having some trouble assimilating that.
Even now, JoAnn met erstwhile boyfriends who *still*
asked, "How's your friend Cynthia?"

JoAnn always said, "Just fine."

"She married yet?"

JoAnn would reply sadly, "Not yet."

And the guy would walk away, undoubtedly looking for a phone to call Cynthia.

* * *

Mina Keeper figured that if Cynthia was that big a fluke in luring Andrew, there was no reason, at all, for her to hang around. It had been proven that Andrew hadn't been distracted by Cynthia. If Cynthia could not catch Andrew's attention, then it must be that Andrew was zonked by…JoAnn?

He'd been concerned with—JoAnn. He *had!*

Mina had thought she's solved JoAnn's rejection of Andrew just with the arrival of Cynthia. Now the Keepers were in deeper with Andrew, suddenly completely involved with and dedicated to…JoAnn!

Quite frankly, that did not make any sense at all.

Mina chewed the inside of her lip and wondered what on earth was going on that she had so little control over *any*thing!

Andrew told the wilted JoAnn, "Do you want to hang around here, or would you go with me to find my dog?"

"Buddy." Her mouth managed that in a first crack in the clearing of her shock.

He nodded, watching her.

She stared at Andrew.

He smiled just a tad and then he inquired, "Want to go along?"

That time, it was she who nodded.

With her agreement, he took her hand and turned away from the blinding Cynthia. Then the two just slid out of the mass of people and went on off.

Andrew was dressed to ride, but he noticed JoAnn was not. So he had to guide JoAnn to her room so that she could change clothing.

He sat on the delicate lady's chair. He found and discreetly read the newspaper given to each room, like a hotel would do.

JoAnn went into the closet in the bath area to choose her shirt and trousers and change into them.

She stared at herself in the mirror. Why hadn't Andrew been zonked by Cynthia? And her naked face looked back at her, still in shock. She ascertained that actually, he was not interested in any woman. That was probably so.

He didn't like women, he hadn't to begin with. Now he was using JoAnn as a shield against other females. That was probably so. She would have to be careful that he didn't hide behind her skirt—slacks, that is, and pretend he was enamored with—her. Yeah. Sure.

Men are really very careful. She had seen men who loved women who didn't have any means. Having used the women, the men had withdrawn from them and married money. Women with money. Had Andrew found out about her grandmother's gift to JoAnn?

That was probably why he'd finally become stringently courteous with her? He knew she had money. How had he known? No one knew. She had never mentioned it for that very reason.

She had never before seen a man reject Cynthia. It hadn't seemed to boggle Cynthia—at *all!*

JoAnn put on makeup. She did her lashes. Then she looked at herself in the bathroom mirror. She exchanged serious regard with the mirror. Soberly, she slowly shook her head, chiding such foolishness.

But she didn't wipe the lipstick all off.

Why was that?

And looking at herself, she knew she wanted Andrew's attentions. She wanted him to hold her close against his hard body. To kiss her. To take her to his room and make love with her.

How come she'd changed her mind about Andrew? Why not her room? He was there right then. Why not strip and walk into her bedroom and stand, startled, and say, "Oh! I forgot you were here!" And she'd put her hands over…her cheeks. And he'd throw the newspaper aside and his breaths would be harsh! Then he'd—

Good gravy, she was a real lamebrain. She was a fool.

There in the bathroom, she considered her mirror image and, under her clothing, she shrugged her shoulders as she accepted that she was a fool.

She left the bathroom and went through the small dressing room. It held the closet on one side for clothing, and the drawers on the other side. The door had a mirror. She watched herself open that door and she went into the bedroom.

There was Andrew, reading the newspaper. He didn't even glance up! If she had been naked, she'd probably have to tear the newspaper from his hands and throw it aside and shock him.

He'd probably frown as he retrieved the paper and he'd say, "I haven't finished that article!"

Umm-hmm.

Andrew rose as she entered. He put the paper on her nightstand by the bed as he said, "Would you save this for me? The maid will probably take my paper when she cleans the room. I'd like to finish that article.''

And JoAnn said, "Yes." Her voice was meek. That made her push out her lower lip as she squinted her eyes a tad. Was she becoming docile? How disgusting. She would not be…docile.

She found her riding gloves and hat. Then without saying another word, she went to her room's hall door.

He was there, and he opened the door for her. He didn't bow, but he did smile at her. "You look great."

She tilted her head back and asked in a deadly manner, "Great? Fat?"

He looked down her body and his eye wrinkles were folded so that no untanned skin showed. He said, "You could lose—"

She gasped.

"—maybe an ounce." He licked his lips and raised his eyes to her face.

Slowly, she was amused. She lifted her eyes to his face and found him watching her with amusement.

This was the man who'd been impossibly rude to her. Could she believe he could change to this delight…and not change back to being as he'd been?

She would see.

She said, "Put on a hat. We're going to look for Buddy."

"Are you sure your guest won't mind you leaving?"

"This is not my house. I did not call her to come

to see me. I think it's more important that I help in looking for a lost dog."

"I'd appreciate the company."

She assured Andrew, "Cynthia will not need to beg for company."

So Andrew tilted his head and asked kindly, "Would she like to join the search?"

That stopped JoAnn. She replied kindly, "It's your search. If you would like others along, it could be wise to do so."

"Wise." He tasted the word.

"The more eyes there are, the better luck you might have." She'd flung down the gauntlet.

Was the "luck" for the dog, or was it for another kind of catching?

Then she said, "We both know the area. Perhaps if you took Cynthia with you, I could find someone else to go with me. That way—let me finish—we could have two searches at the same time."

That was a gauntlet down if ever there'd been one.

Andrew wasn't exactly sure how to handle this fire-brand. He looked at her, and he knew he wanted to be with her. She was someone he needed to know. Another woman wasn't what he wanted. Just her.

Very kindly, he said to JoAnn, "Maybe one of the men could take Cynthia out as they looked around for Buddy?"

She responded, "I'm not that acquainted with the crew. I don't know what their schedules are. You could ask one of the adult Keepers. I'll go on out."

Seriously, he asked, "Wait for me." Well, that

wasn't a question. It was an order. He told her to wait for him.

She looked at her watch and said, "I'll give you fifteen minutes to get back here."

He grinned and went to her door. She noted then that it was closed. A real gentleman did not close room doors when he wasn't married to the lady. She tilted her chin up and said, "My door was closed."

"I didn't want anybody else in here."

"—so you could read in peace?"

His grin began. His eye-corn-wrinkles closed up and he said, "Yeah." Very amused.

She said flippantly, "Shame on you." And she opened the door. She said, "While you're setting up the other searchers, I'll just go on."

"Where will you be?"

And she readily replied quite seriously, offhand and dismissively, "Out in the third quarter. To the east of here. We've done the north and west." She started through the door.

He said, "Drop portions of your shirt. Birds eat bread."

She stopped and looked back in order to soberly consider him. "Yes." With that nothing reply, she went on off.

But Andrew contacted Cynthia and she was concerned for the dog and agreed to get someone to go out with her to search for the dog. Andrew did a very good drawing of the dog and gave search directions on a piece of paper.

Cynthia was not only concerned, she was eager for

the search. She liked dogs. She didn't want her aunt to spend the day racking Cynthia's brain for gossip or who all was doing what all. And she was ready to get out of the house.

"Get a hat," Andrew called back to Cynthia.

"I'm a TEXAN, boy, I know them thar things." But Cynthia's words were lost; Andrew was already gone.

And having been thoroughly informed by Mrs. Keeper, Cynthia thought, "...with JoAnn. Andrew was anxious to be with JoAnn. How interesting." Andrew had been in a hurry. Knowing JoAnn as she did, Cynthia smiled. Smart girl! She was handling this odd man just right.

Cynthia tilted her head. Probably JoAnn was the only woman around who knew how to bring such a man up-to-date. She would.

Then Cynthia went off to garner whatall *wo*men would be delighted to spend the day out and about with her.

Cynthia was fun. She was alert. She garnered the women who were, indeed, delighted to be included. She ended up with at least a dozen. And they were good-lookers. Not only did they look good, but they'd also look for the dog.

Cynthia's bunch called and whistled and scared the hell out of a whole herd of longhorns who were precious and cared for and *nobody ever* startled them...but the women did.

The herd stampeded. They did. With their great

horns and those low hanging things on their stomachs in jeopardy, they were fragile.

Now how is a longhorn crew going to get hostile to a bunch of darling women? The women were shocked and wanted to help regather the herd. They did! One of the men took off his hat as he tried to control his excited horse, and he said, "Thanks anyway. We'll see you all later and tell you what all these beasts do."

Then he put his hat back on his own head and slid the catch up the strings to keep his Stetson on his head. He rode off in the dust after the whistling and calling of earnest men, almost covered by the sounds of thudding hooves.

It was a very stimulating encounter for the women, and they were quite animated.

The men had vanished into the dust.

Cynthia had a very difficult time not throwing back her head and howling with laughter. But the women were very involved. They really looked for the dog. They whistled and called and *looked*. They were quite earnest.

No one found the dog Buddy.

There was no clue at *all* as to where he could be.

So Cynthia extended her visit in order to help look for the lost dog. She was given a room that was marvelous, and she had all the attention she could possibly endure. She was kind, busy, and she knew exactly what she needed and how to organize the groups.

The next day's hunt was equally intense.

But they didn't find the dog...anywhere. They whistled and called and looked, but Buddy was nowhere around, in that area, at all.

So Cynthia went home. She was not a loser and it irritated her that she had engagements that she needed to fulfill. That's what she got for being so perfect. She told Mina, "I'll be back."

With Cynthia gone, everybody took a day off. They were exhausted. The crew chided Mina Keeper, "That Cynthia is hell-bent! She rode us down to a nub!"

Another hand protested, "Huntin' isn't riding that-away."

And the first hand retorted, "We wasn't *riding*. We was *lookin'!*"

Mina Keeper replied, "Yes." And she went to her room and to her bed with a cool cloth for her forehead.

There would be a snowball in hell before Mina called on Cynthia again.

The crew lost no time in hunting—farther. They looked for any evidence of anyone being on the tableland. They had not forgotten the enormous bullet that had killed the pilgrim Andrew Parson's horse. And a serious group spread out and went on beyond, still looking, and also trying to solve who had fired that shot to kill the horse under the limping Andrew Parsons.

The female group was so cheerful and calling to each other, in their search for Buddy, they had irritated the very hell out of Andrew. He was glad Cynthia was gone.

He said to JoAnn, "Now we can quietly go around and look for Buddy."

JoAnn replied, "We were lucky to find those people and let them help us."

Andrew noted that she felt a partner in the search. Did she feel like a partner with—him?

She said, "The only place left, where the dog could be, is in the town."

It wasn't actually a "town," it was just the casually bunched houses where the crew lived, but they had a grocery, a library!...but no town hall—as yet.

Somehow thinking of Buddy being in *town* had not occurred to Andrew. Thoughtfully, he said, "Yeah."

The dog would go where he could find a garbage can. He would need to eat. No. Buddy would not do that. He was a good hunter. He wouldn't eat from a garbage can.

Andrew considered his life of obsolescence. He knew more than she did about Buddy. He said, "We'll see." He didn't want to discourage her. He wanted to be with her. To share. How strange. He looked at JoAnn and saw her as a miracle.

Andrew considered when had he ever thought a woman was a—miracle? Handy. Yeah. Interesting. Yeah. Available. Yeah. But JoAnn as a miracle. He'd never tangled with a miracle before then. He frowned and chewed his lower lip.

She thought he was discarding being with her. It

was his choice. Damn. Well, now was as good a time as any. She—

"Would you go into town with me? We could ask around and see if anyone's seen Buddy."

He wanted her along? Well, he probably needed somebody with him. This was a hard time for a man who'd lost such a dog.

So the next morning, after breakfast, the two mounted their horses and with no anticipation, at *all*, they rode gently into the living area just south of the ranch house.

There was some distance. Maybe a couple of blocks if it was a city. The Keepers kept thinking their offspring would build houses near to theirs. None of the last two generations had done that. They'd gone off on their own, leaving the rancher of them, at home. None of the others wanted to share. They were an Independent Bunch.

Keepers were thataway. Generally one would stay. He'd be the jewel of the bunch. The one who wanted to work the ranch. Like Tom Keeper. He was the one to keep there. He was the one who was interested in the Place.

He loved it. If he didn't keep having to go look for a woman, he wouldn't have to leave the place. But he wanted children. So he wanted a woman who'd not mind living out there.

He'd found a couple along the way who would have been willing to share a place in town, but none wanted to live so far out on the tableland.

* * *

So it was Tom who went with Andrew and JoAnn into the little settlement of hands and families to look for the dog Buddy.

Andrew said, "He's a hunter."

Tom nodded. "We'll find out if he's been around here."

Neither Tom nor JoAnn inquired as to why the dog had vanished.

Tom suggested, "Let's go by Rip's first. He's a pilot and knows Buddy. He flew him out to you."

Andrew nodded as he replied, "I remember he kept the dog while I was in hospital."

Tom mentioned, "Yeah." Then Tom remembered Andrew's sister. She had moved in with Rip. Tom wondered if going to Rip's house was maybe not a good idea. He said, "We can go to Paul's and ask if he's seen Buddy. Paul has the eyes of a hawk."

And Andrew said, "I'd like to see Rip. He was very kind to us."

Tom became a little anxious. Did Andrew know that Lu was living with Rip? She'd been to the big house quite a few times. Tom couldn't remember her being there much lately. She might not know the dog was missing. But she would understand her brother's probable response to her staying with Rip.

So Tom sweat. How could he ask if Andrew knew that his sister was staying with Rip? How could he approach that subject? He wouldn't say anything. He'd be surprised.

Tom asked, "You got a gun on you?"

Andrew was startled. "No. Why?"

Tom said, "We have a law about the guns being worn around here."

"You're wearing one."

"I'm a Keeper. I can do that."

"Isn't that taking on rules that are obsolete?"

It was an obsolete man who asked that.

Tom replied, "It's in the books. Thataway, the owner is in charge and can control."

"That's obsolete." How strange such a man could label someone else as being so.

JoAnn said nothing. But she considered the two men.

Each man wondered which side she was on.

Gradually, with their walking horses, the trio came in sight of Rip's place. It was sparkling with new paint and looked cared for and neat.

—and on the porch, in charge, was...Buddy. He, too, looked neat and cared for. The dog looked at the approaching trio, and he went inside the dog door and disappeared.

Andrew pointed and said, "That was Buddy!"

And Tom inquired, "Why would he vanish so quickly?"

"I don't know. But it *was* my dog!"

JoAnn soothed, "It may have been a very similar one?"

"No. That's Buddy." He whistled.

Nothing happened. The dog door stayed closed.

Tom said, "I'll go up and see if Rip's home."

"Yeah." And Andrew got off his horse and dropped the reins for it to stay there.

Tom dismounted and repeated sternly, "I'll go see if Rip's home."

Andrew was logical. "That's my dog."

"We'll see." Tom then said firmly, "You wait here. Understand?"

So Andrew, being the independent he was, whistled for the dog.

They stood there. Nothing happened. No dog appeared.

Tom put his hand on Andrew's chest and said firmly, "You are to wait right here. Do you understand me?"

"A dog's a dog. That one is mine."

"He didn't want to come to you. You are to wait here until I find out what is going on. I mean that."

JoAnn said, "He'll stay with me out of rampant courtesy since I would be alone out here, clear out on the street."

Andrew looked up at JoAnn. He considered her. Then he said to Tom, "I beg your pardon."

Tom nodded once and walked up to the porch steps. He glanced back to be sure he wasn't being followed, then he went to the door and knocked. He dreaded that it would be Lu who responded to the door knock, but there was no reply.

Buddy did not emerge from his door.

Tom called, "Nobody's home."

Andrew replied, "Buddy's there. Let me come talk to him."

So Tom tapped on the dog door and pushed it gently. It was blocked. The dog was sitting silently behind the door, blocking it.

Tom crossed the porch and went down the stairs as he said, "Buddy declines to come out. No human is home. Rip is probably flying. I'll call in and see what his schedule is."

With serious eyes, Andrew echoed, "He—declines—coming out?"

"He's blocked the dog door."

Andrew was shocked. "Well, I'll be damned."

And JoAnn commented, "Very probably."

Seven

Tom Keeper was a man who knew animals. He dealt in animals, he lived with them, he sold them. He understood them. Standing in front of the pilot Rip's house, Tom told his guest, Andrew Parsons, "Go back to the ranch."

"My dog is here."

"He ran away from you and *came* here. The fact that he's blocked the dog door shows that he is not interested in going with you. Animals need to have the same rights as a human. He does not want to be with you. Go back to the Keeper ranch."

Now, did Tom's identifying the ranch as Keeper territory mean to inform Andrew that he was a guest? That he was not at home. That Andrew was not in territory that he commanded. That he was a pilgrim in a strange land?

Probably.

Tom was stubborn and dangerous. He had said what he wanted, now he waited for Andrew to obey.

Andrew...obey? How droll.

But watching, still on her horse, was JoAnn Murray.

Ahhhh. Now, how was Andrew going to solve his problem? He could discard Tom and do as he chose. He could obey what Tom had demanded.

And Tom *had* demanded such obedience. He had not asked, he had told Andrew what he could not do. And what was expected of him.

That was what wobbled Andrew. He did not want to be told what to do.

So it was JoAnn who said, "Tom is logical. The dog has been missing for some time. Buddy. Isn't that his name? He doesn't want to confront you at this time. That is especially clear. He chose to go inside. Now Tom is giving you time to consider all this."

Besides Tom, JoAnn was logical.

There was a long silence.

JoAnn said softly, "Do it."

Now the two watched Andrew to see if *he* could be logical.

Andrew wondered where tact had gone. It was no longer a manner. He had been—told—what he was to do, and it irked the hell out of him. Especially in front of JoAnn.

But it was obvious that JoAnn thought Tom was acting exactly right. It was *Andrew* who was the sticker-burr in all this.

Even his dog had hidden. Buddy had taken one

look at Andrew before he had gone inside and blocked the dog door. Just that was very telling.

So Andrew asked, "Is he all right?"

Tom said, "He looked okay. Rip would take good care of him."

"This…Rip is the one who brought the dog to me when I was trapped under the dead horse and to the hospital when I was there. Why would Rip keep Buddy, now?"

Tom was gentle. "You forget that the dog left you and came to Rip."

After a time, Andrew agreed, "Yes."

JoAnn said, "Let's go back to the Keepers' place until this can be settled. You should be relieved the dog is safe…here."

And slowly, after some silence, Andrew said, "Yes. We've been through a great deal together, the dog and I."

"Then give him room." JoAnn said that softly.

Andrew looked up at JoAnn who still sat her horse. Then Andrew took the first step up to the porch as he said to Tom, "Let me…speak to Buddy."

"No tricks. I'd shoot you."

Andrew was briefly startled, then he smiled. "I won't do anything but talk to him just for a minute."

Tom said stonily, "I'm watching you."

It was interesting to Andrew that he was extremely conscious of his back, which was exposed and very vulnerable. Tom had said he'd shoot Andrew. He wouldn't lie. Lying wasn't in Tom.

And Andrew remembered the telling of the story of Tom taking pit dogs bought—at the fighting pits—

by some indignant woman. Tom had parceled the
dogs out among friends. One dog was not a friend
but a hostile, fighting dog. Tom had that dog guarding
an acre the prairie dogs had taken over as their land.

Then as Andrew crossed the porch slowly, he recalled that Tom had taken some female dog out to
the guard of the prairie dog land and given the bitch
to him. The pit dog had gently accepted the bitch as
his, and she had been willing.

Just that made Andrew consider what Tom was doing for Buddy, right then. The dogs were free. Buddy
was free to choose.

Andrew squatted down beside the dog door that
Buddy sat behind to block it. A smart dog who could
handle anything.

Andrew said, "Buddy." And there was no reply.
So Andrew pushed his hand softly against the dog
door and it was indeed blocked. Andrew was strong
enough to swat the door and move the dog, but Andrew could not go through that slot himself.

Andrew said, "I'm glad you're okay. Rip is a good
man. You're a good dog. I've missed you. Take care
of yourself."

Then Andrew slowly turned, left the porch and returned to the two who waited for him. It was probably
the tears that had sneaked onto Andrew's eyelashes
that caught both Tom's and JoAnn's attention. Were
the tears for losing the dog…or were they frustration
because Buddy had chosen sides?

The last of the three humans remounted his horse.
The three were silent, going back to the ranch. Tom

Keeper noted there was no offer of casual conversation. It was a very serious thing that had occurred. All three were aware of that.

Probably the one most aware was Andrew? That alone was a surprise. Was he considering himself? Or did he think of the dog's rejecting conduct? That would be interesting to know.

As they approached the barns, Andrew asked JoAnn, "Stay with me?" Well, it wasn't actually a question. He just did not want to be alone. He wanted to be with her.

She looked over at Andrew. Being on a horse instead of driving a car, one could look around and reply and let the horse just go along by itself.

JoAnn noted Andrew was stressed. She responded to his plea, "Yes." She was very serious. She didn't blink her lashes or smile or wiggle or anything.

Within the building area, the silent Tom touched his hat to JoAnn and said, "I'll be in touch." And he rode his horse at a gallop in another direction. He was gone.

Andrew said thoughtfully, "I ticked him off."

"Yep."

Andrew looked at her as he asked carefully watching, "—and you?"

"I've known you better than Tom. I understand you. You're—"

"We have known each other quite well." His words were spoken in satisfaction.

She ignored his interruption. "—a throwback and believe you are a rule in yourself. You handled—"

"Throwback?"

"—the occasion as you would without considering any one else. You—"

"I'm inconsiderate?"

"—were lucky Tom Keeper was along and could outdraw on you. He had control. He—"

"Control? There was no *need*—"

"—was kind in not beaning you with his revolver."

Andrew turned his head and looked at JoAnn in shock. "I was very careful and considerate."

"You were a nerd."

In a hostile manner, Andrew snarled, "I'm not so obsolete that I don't know that word. It was used clear back when I was in England. I was called one then!"

Calmly, JoAnn replied, "You were the stranger. All those isolated boys could pick on you and feel as if they belonged, but you did not."

That silenced Andrew. He rode silently to the barn and just sat on his horse, as he looked back in his mind and remembered. "Yes."

He got off his horse and almost took his into the barn, but he remembered JoAnn was still on her horse. She just sat and watched him. He went to her side and looked up at her. He asked, "How did I find you?"

"You'll never know."

She slid her feet from the stirrups and swung her leg over the horse's neck. Then without any warning at all, she slid off the horse, allowing Andrew to catch her.

He did.

He held her seriously, looking at her face with naked eyes. He pulled her to him and kissed her very seriously and with emotion—not even noticing that the horse walked on off into the barn.

As he lifted his mouth very gently, intensely focused on her, she said, "Your horse needs his saddle off."

He was startled for a minute. Then he nodded. "When I kissed you that seriously, how could you be aware of what the hell the *horse* was doing?"

She watched him and her smile came slowly. Her eyes narrowed. She said, "I noticed the kiss."

And he huffed. "Well, I should hope so! That was my best try ever!"

She smiled wider, more gently and pushed his hair back with her gloved hand. "You're something."

His entire body tingling, he noted that she was releasing herself and gently turning away. Reluctant to leave her or have her leave him, he went along beside her. "This 'something' you mention. Is that good or bad?"

"Devastating."

"I'm...ruining you?" He was upset.

"Yep."

"I don't mean to—"

She was finishing her sentence: "—for any other man."

He had to lean his head back to breathe at all. His eyes were briefly closed by the wave of sensation that flooded him. He urged, "Let's check out the hay in the loft."

She smiled like a cat that's just finished a mouse. Her eyes blinked slowly. She said, "We have to unsaddle the horses."

He frowned at her and scolded. "How come you can remember what all *else* needs doing?"

"In another life I was a horse?"

He took in more air and he didn't need any more air. He watched her walk past him, leading her horse. He looked around for his and it was gone!

He followed her into the stable saying, "My horse—" And there it was, still saddled and eating from the hay.

She thought he was indicating that he first needed to unsaddle his own horse, and she just said, "Yes."

So the two did that. He told her, "Let me do yours."

But she crippled his tongue by replying, "I can. You'll have enough to do with just me."

She didn't even look up. She just went along unbuckling her saddle and relieving the horse of the burden. The horse shook herself and went to the trough to suck in water.

JoAnn turned on the water spigot, leaned over holding her hat and drank sideways from the water.

She looked up, and Andrew was watching. She asked, "Want some?" and indicated the water flowing from the spigot.

He came to her and put his hand on her neck. Then he bent and drank from the same spigot.

He lifted his head and just looked at her. He said,

"All of the problems of being trapped under the horse and being in the hospital and losing Buddy were worth finding you."

She tilted her head a couple of times. "I'm better than a dog?"

"Be quiet." And he took her into his arms and held her against his aching body. He groaned.

"I haven't been in a hayloft since I was about twelve."

"Who were you with?"

How male of him. "Five little girls my own age and we made tunnels in the hay—"

"That's very dangerous."

"That's odd. Two cowboys came in and heard us laughing and read us the riot act. They were appalled we'd never known about collapsing hay." She tilted her head. "We'd had such a good time."

"Nobody smothered."

"No."

"You were lucky."

She looked up at the hayloft and said, "Let's see if there's enough for a...bed."

He hyperventilated.

She went to the ladder and glanced back to see if he followed. He was very serious.

He said, "I have no protection for you."

She smiled. "I do."

And he gasped. "Why...you *scarlet* woman! My daddy *told* me about women like you."

She laughed so softly as she watched him come toward her.

He crowded her, and she allowed that. She lifted her face and her eyes were slitted and wicked.

So he kissed her. It was so gentle and careful. She wondered how many women he'd had. He was so careful of her. His hands were so gentle.

He said, "Let's get up there so you can see the hay?"

"Good idea." She put her boot onto the step and her mouth was even with his. She kissed him.

"If you stood on a step each time, you might save my neck."

She laughed in her throat the way a woman does with a man she likes.

She liked him. He rubbed his face against hers like a cat. He said, "You like me."

"Ummmm."

"What sort of reply is that?" His voice was deep and soft and just for her.

And she whispered, "I want you."

He rolled his head back so that he could try to breathe, and he said, "I think I can lift you in my arms and *jump* up into the loft."

"I might muss my hair."

He put his arms around her as he said, "How come is it that you of all the people here, can like me so easily?"

"You are unique. You're asinine and—"

"I am not, either! I'm a darling man!"

"I'm waiting to see if you go back to being rude."

He watched her in his arms. "I was rude to you?"

"Yes."

"I beg your pardon. I didn't realize I was being

rude. Was it when we first met? Yes. I do that to protect myself. I've been rejected so much that I need a shield.''

"Who rejected you?"

"People. Now...Buddy. I've been abandoned. Help me."

"I'll see."

Carefully, he asked, "What will you...see."

"If I want to be with you."

"I'll be very careful."

She smiled. "...for a while?"

Then he grinned at her and raised his eyebrows in a smug manner. "We'll see how eager you are. How much you want me."

"Yes."

Then he asked gently, "Are you sure?"

"I was at this ladder before you even mentioned making love with me."

"Well, thank goodness you didn't say making love *to* you. That would probably mean you would lie down like a stick and not help me at *all*."

She laughed in a smothered gasp and loved the comment. "I'll wiggle a little."

"I love...I *think* I'd like to ride a wiggling woman."

"Since I'll be on the bottom, I'll go on up first."

He put his hand on her bottom. "Need a boost?"

"No." Then she gasped rather elaborately. "Can you get up the ladder okay?"

He considered the ladder. It was handmade, put together, nailed on risers along two four-by-fours. He said with very little conviction, "It could hold me."

"Let's try. I'll go first. Wait until I'm off the ladder. Two on it might not be a good idea."

"Don't burrow into the hay. We aren't going up yonder to play hide-and-seek."

"Not this time."

She was so quick. She was so quick and sly and her smile was so—wicked! She was the stuff of dreams. He groaned and put his head back again. He said, "Hustle up." And he patted her bottom.

So she went on up and disappeared. That rattled him and he was right on up the ladder and immediately looking. No man who has a willing woman wants her out of his reach.

He couldn't see her. But he could hear the movement of the hay. He whispered rather loudly, "Be careful. Don't get smothered."

"I'm just over here."

He turned, and she was closer to the front of the barn and she was—adjusting the hay.

She said, "No birds here."

He had to laugh and he did that silently. There had to be hands around, and they might hear the two lovers.

She was a lover. How long had it been since he'd had a woman like her? Had he ever? She wasn't only logical, she was pliant and interested…in *him!*

It wouldn't be a wam, bam, thank you ma'am rush. She wanted attention. In a hayloft?

Well, he'd just see to it.

Andrew watched as JoAnn stripped naked in a ray of sun. She almost smiled at him.

He was breathing strangely. He was riveted. He was out of his clothes in no time at *all.*

She wanted to roll on the condom. They had a discussion on that and he finally said, "Next time." And he did it by himself.

He was so body hungry that he couldn't wait. He carefully entered her and his sex was rampant. He just went ahead and only hesitated in order for her body to catch up with the want in his. So he was clever and patient enough that they hit the high mark together...and they floated down from wherever they'd hung in midair, still throbbing with their ecstasy.

He was almost appalled that he had been so greedy. He groaned and breathed and lay on her in a collapse. His hand patted her head. He shook his head slowly as he tried to control his breathing.

Under him, she lay silent.

He managed to drag himself up on his elbows and let her uneven but crushed chest breathe. His head hung down beside hers. He said in carefully spaced, breathing words, "I wish—I could've—lasted longer."

She said, "Wow."

He cautioned carefully, "Don't—make me—laugh. I'm—concen-trat-ing on breathing."

"You're doing okay."

"Don't—be—sassy."

"I haven't stuck out my tongue like you did with that awesome thing that was waggling around in your drawers."

He laughed and rolled off her to lie beside her with

his eyes closed and his body and appendages as limp as rags, but he held her hand.

She rolled over until she could look down at him. "Do men all collapse after something like that?"

"Why—do—you ask?"

"I just wondered if all men are like you. If I didn't know you were in good health, I'd be panicked you were in danger of a heart attack or something."

"This was—your first?"

"Well, yeah. How experienced are you?"

"I don't remember—ever—doing anything—so drastic—before—in all my—life. I may well die—right here—naked—like this. It was—worth—it. I may—go to sleep."

She laughed.

He snorted.

She giggled.

His face was relaxed and he was *out!* It was real.

She turned over on her side and put a hand between her tender cheek and the rough hay. She watched him. He really was out cold!

He slept for almost an hour. The only thing that wakened him was one of the ranch hands delivering a horse to the barn and finding another one who was rested.

They were silent in the loft. They heard the hand whistling to himself as he worked to relieve the first horse and saddle the other one. He slapped the side of the first one and said, "You're free—enough. Don't drink too much water right off, hear?"

Then he got on the other horse and thudded away over the hard land.

In the loft, on the flattened hay, she was curled up watching Andrew.

He told her, "You're amazing."

"You needed a woman."

"Yeah. But I got you. I can't believe it yet."

"You need me again, already?"

"I'm not sure I can perform as well, but it would be nice to see if I wasn't dreaming you."

She rolled onto him.

That triggered him so that he whooshed air. He was rigid again.

She said, "You're too easy. You ought to protest or gasp or chide me."

"No."

She laughed softly, so amused. "I'm no help this time. You drained me."

"Did I hurt you?" He was concerned.

"Naw. I'm contented."

"I'm not."

She laughed softly, lying back on the hay to have the room for such an action. It was difficult to laugh softly or to smother a laugh. Especially when they were where they were.

He kissed her very softly, but he put his hand where he wanted it.

She chided, "You sneaky man. You thought if you kissed me again, I wouldn't notice what *else* you were doing."

Moving his finger inside her, he put his face on her

breasts and gently moved it over her nipples. He said a whole lot of *m*'s.

She sighed. "I suppose I was rash in allowing you one contact. Now you'll think you can do all *sorts* of things to my body!"

He made agreeing sounds.

She shifted so that he could reach farther. She moved her chest and his mouth captured one eager nub.

She had never allowed any such contact before and she was so thrilled by him that she wondered what all she'd missed! She made gasping sounds and her legs and arms were restless.

He rolled over on top of her and said, "Do tell me that you have another condom."

She shook her head sadly. "It's in my room."

He stopped. He breathed. He said, "Let's go to your room."

She grinned and said, "I'll probably get there first."

"I'll be right behind you."

And he quite easily showed her exactly how that could be.

She gasped and moved and tilted her head back. Then she turned her head and he kissed her. She was backward on his lap, his hands were on her breasts, and she could feel the size of him under her.

She said, "Let's go to my room."

"Yeah."

But he squeezed and kissed and rubbed her until she was just about wild.

Then he lifted her effortlessly and expected her to

stand...in straw? And he straightened up, pulled her to him and kissed her entirely witless. Then he expected her to dress!

She fumbled.

He assisted her. He knew absolutely nothing about women's clothing. She had to switch the pant legs so that the zipper was in the front. She showed him the buttons were on the wrong side of her shirt. She ended up tying the tails of her shirt together and just letting it go.

Her bra was in her pocket with her socks. Her boots were on bare feet. She ran her fingers through her hair and got rid of—well—most of the straw. And she thought she was ready to be in the public eye.

She looked at Andrew.

He was stuffing his shirt into his trousers. Then he pulled out the tails and let them hang. He pulled on his boots and stood up.

She said, "Anybody who sees us will know where we've been and why."

His grin slowly widened. He said, "Okay."

She sighed and looked off to one side. She told him, "I'll go first. And in twenty minutes, you come to my room. Okay?"

His face crumpled all screwed up in astonishment. *"Twenty minutes!"*

She looked at him with sober consideration. "Make it ten."

She left, and he reached for her but she dodged out of his hands and grinned. "I'll see you soon."

And he growled.

* * *

As far as they could tell, no one saw them cross the yard and go to her room. No one was anywhere around.

At her room, she opened her door for him and no one else was in the hall. She ordered her supper on the house phone to be delivered in one hour.

Then she smiled at him. It was a Cheshire cat's smile. She asked, "Can I use you again, this soon?"

"Oh, yes."

"You are shockingly willing. How basic of you."

He just came over and kissed her. He said, "How did I ever find you?"

"Mrs. Keeper sent for me. I was to tame you. You were such a beast when I first arrived. I almost abandoned you altogether."

"I'm glad you didn't."

"How can I tell whether you're just sexually hungry, or if you are ensnared by me?"

He considered, tilting his head and observing her in a very theatrical manner. He replied to her question, "We'll see."

That made her laugh.

And *that's* what snared her to him. What other woman would have laughed with such a reply from a man? She would have been either careful or she would have worried. JoAnn laughed.

So they talked. They talked about what they wanted in life. He wasn't entirely sure. But she listened to him. And when it was time for dinner to be delivered, she put him in the hall of double closets between the room and her bath, and she closed the door into the room.

She accepted the meal.

The deliverer commented, "You must be starving."

And she replied, "It's been a long day. I'll probably go right to bed."

She said *that* to someone else and kept a straight *face!*

Did the server hear Andrew's quickly silenced choke in the inside hall behind the closed door? Who cared?

With the waiter gone, Andrew came out of the inside hall and chided, "You're wicked."

And she replied, "Yes. That's why I chose you. Like likes like. You're like me. Masculine, but wicked."

He lifted his chin and looked at her over his cheekbones. He said, "I'll have you know that I was raised in a very strange house. My father had me in school in Britain? He couldn't assume I'd be taught in English at a farther place. We don't communicate."

"How foolish of him."

"I don't mind. We are not acquainted."

But Andrew didn't fool JoAnn—at all.

Eight

JoAnn considered Andrew. She sighed without seeming to do so. What a man does to make a woman think he's macho. It's really pretty stupid. That attitude wasn't current. There were the Romans who used men to fight other beasts to entertain in the Colosseum.

Thoughtfully, JoAnn wondered: Was Andrew such a creature? Had he chosen to be obsolete in order to attract attention to himself? To be on display and therefore watched?

JoAnn considered.

His father not only ignored Andrew, but he also had sent his son clear across the sea to another land where he grew up totally isolated from the family. Andrew had been in school in winter and he'd traveled the European continent with a guide in the summer, holiday months.

What sort of waggle did that cause in Andrew's opinion of himself? What sort of wimp was his mother? What sort of genes would emotionally cripple his children? JoAnn decided that she would meet his father and his wimpish mother and observe them.

It was only then that JoAnn learned quite by accident that Andrew's sister, Lu, was living with the ranch pilot Rip! Rip was the one with whom the dog Buddy had taken shelter.

And so had Andrew's sister. Did Andrew know that his sister was living with Rip? Was his knowing Lu was with Rip why Andrew had been reasonable about the dog staying at Rip's with Andrew's sister?

Even then, Andrew had not caught up to time. Did JoAnn want the challenge of bringing him up-to-date? Andrew certainly knew sex. But sex had been around for a whole long time. What else did Andrew know that was current?

Andrew had been kind to the dog and left him where the dog wanted to be. He hadn't dragged Buddy back to himself. He'd allowed the dog to decide.

Of course, at the time, there was Tom's drawn gun on Andrew. That could quite easily have convinced Andrew to be logical.

Thoughtfully, JoAnn turned and observed the watching Andrew. He sat in a chair in her room. His eyes were on her avidly. He was again triggered. Would he be that attentive when he was sated? Or would he discard her only to hunt her down when he was again in need?

JoAnn smiled just a tad and asked Andrew, "What are you thinking?" She knew darned good and well what he was thinking. She just wanted to know what he'd say and how he'd say it.

His smile vulnerable, he said softly, "You're so kind."

JoAnn laughed. She asked, "Because I lie down and spread my legs for you?"

Without changing his expression, Andrew replied, "Because you're logical. You understand. You say what I need to hear. I've never been taught how to be with other people. In England at the school, I was different.

"I had no other choice but to be what I was. I traveled as did the people long ago. I could then be—different enough to be noticed. I've been ignored by my family. I don't know how to live. You could guide me—logically."

JoAnn didn't huff or verbally push him away, she listened.

Andrew said carefully, "It's very strange to be somewhere as a child, and be...different."

JoAnn began to really dislike his father and mother. What asinine people they must be. But she also knew she had to be logical with Andrew. If she comforted him or took his side, he could become hostile to his family.

She would need to be an arbitrator. Someone who is on neither side. She would listen.

She couldn't reply what she felt, so she did as she'd

decided and she listened. She asked careful questions so that she understood Andrew better. "Are you good at the English games?"

"Oh, yes. They were careful that we all played and knew what we were doing. That direction was in the classes also. I was different. No other 'Yankee' was anywhere around. They called everyone from over here...Yankees. It was an adjustment for me."

Then he said thoughtfully, "No one needed me. They weren't rejecting as much as they just didn't realize I was there."

"The teachers didn't notice?"

"They were kind. They spoke to me but there wasn't the open camaraderie there is here." He corrected that thoughtfully, "I felt—different."

JoAnn's heart squeezed in silent sympathy. She despised his selfish parents. She'd shrivel them into pits.

She went and sat on Andrew's easily excited lap. She slid her gentle fingers into his hair.

His eyes were vulnerable and his breathing changed. He said, "How come you did that?"

"It's a caress."

He said, "Oh."

Then he asked, "If I put my hand like that, is that a caress?"

"On that particular area, it's okay when we're by ourselves, but with someone else around, it would be salacious."

"Wow! I'm being...salacious?"

"Stridently. Anytime you're within three feet of me."

He licked his lips carefully and even bit into his

lower lip a tad. Then he said, "Why, I hadn't noticed—being salacious. How...shocking." His tone was all wrong.

She said, "Hah!"

Now, Andrew had never had the teasing and sassiness of a woman in all his life. It was new to him. He was so charmed by it. By her. By JoAnn's response. By her tolerance. By her chidings and limits. By her delicious laughter. It was so soft and—intimate.

She shivered his insides and about wrecked his sex. Could it grow bigger? It was shocking to him. It was so eager! He laughed. "You keep this up, and I'll have to carry Freeman in a wheelbarrow."

"Freeman?" Her smile was gentle and filled with not understanding.

"That's the name I have for my, uh, sex? It's obviously male, and he sure as hell has a mind of his own. He wants you at the worst possible times."

She put her head back and laughed so softly and so amused.

Andrew's voice was vulnerable. "I love the way you laugh when you're with me. You're so gentle and tolerant that—"

She straightened. "Tolerant? I'm—tolerant? Balderdash! I either agree or I strongly disagree and—"

"At the pilot's house, you allowed me to obey Tom without losing my dignity. Your words were chosen to kindly chide me and to allow me freedom. I'll never forget that."

"I understood you."

He gasped, "Do you have trouble with your family?"

"No. But I've witnessed clashes between people that I never could understand."

He said gently, "I'm so glad I found you."

"You're not like other men. Remember when we first met? You were about as rude as you could—"

"You terrified me."

She was startled. "Why did you think that?"

"I didn't know how to handle you."

She lifted her eyebrows and shrugged nicely as she commented, "Well, you've been handling me pretty well ever since!"

"You noticed."

She laughed as she sat on his lap and ruffled his hair.

So they kissed and murmured and laughed softly and went to her bed and did it again.

A few nights later, as John and Mina Keeper were getting ready for bed, and Mina was winding her curls again, John said, "I haven't seen either Andrew or JoAnn in several days. Have they left?"

Mina took a pick out of her mouth and put it in her hair. She replied, "No. They're becoming acquainted."

"So *that's* what it's called now."

"Hush."

John asked, "Do you agree with people shacking up before they're married?"

"We did."

John put a hand on his undershirted chest and exclaimed in a very soft manner, "We...did? How shocking! Was I asleep and you took advantage of me?"

"Never. You were always using all nine hands."

John was surprised. "I have...nine hands?"

"I counted."

"How come I didn't have...ten? An equal number and balance. For a horse man, balance is important."

"I bit off the one when you first accosted me."

"So *that's* what happened to it. Um-hmmm. I remember that, now. You were a handful, as I recall. I had a terrible time trying to get you under me."

"A crude, uncouth man."

"You loved it."

"Hush!"

"Why?"

"Some of the kids might hear you and realize what hungry gropers we—you are."

"How are the love birds doing?" John asked.

"Okay."

Cautiously, John inquired, "Will they...make it?"

"I think they already have."

"How shocking." Then John sighed in a blue manner as he asked his wife, "What are we gonna do about Tom? He's getting long in the tooth. And he's supposed to be the one who supplies the next generation."

Mina said kindly, "We'll see."

"You've gotten Cynthia out here how many times, and he's never even noticed."

She finally admitted, "All the women I've dragged

out here were primarily for Tom. Matching them was getting rid of them because Tom wasn't interested.''

"He's...okay...isn't he? Masculine and so forth?"

"No problem."

"He's gonna be *thirty-six* this year!"

"I know."

"Should I look around for him?"

Mina replied pretty fast, "No!"

"Well, if I can help you in this, I would try."

"Men are very strange characters."

He gasped, "*Men* are? I thought it was w— Other people."

"So. You think women are strange?"

"They sure as hell baffle me." Then he added hastily, "How come you're a woman and you're logical."

"I've taught you to recognize logic."

"Oh."

She was on the very *edge* of hilarity.

He sighed and hugged her gently. "I was lucky to find you. Do you know I love you?"

"I don't recall ever hearing you say something like that."

"Your memory's flawed. I've told you at least every week."

She mentioned gently, "Perhaps that isn't often enough to remember what you've said."

"I suppose. Be quiet and I'll tell you now."

She was silent.

"You asleep?"

"Listening."

"I love you, Mina."

She put her hand on his face and then she kissed him.

Then John asked Mina, "What are we going to do about Tom? He's here. He'll stay here, but how can we find him a wife? He never leaves the place anymore—"

"Let's ask."

And her husband told Mina, "This is man talk, I'll handle it."

While she shivered in appalled terror, she said, "Yes."

And he would! He'd chide Tom and bully him and ruin *every*thing.

The shooting of Andrew Parson's horse still lay under all their skins. A horse is precious to TEXANS.

With all the other things that were going on at the ranch and in the little town, nobody forgot that they were in danger. People live in fear just so long. Two things happen. Constant pressure causes resistance. And if someone is pushing, but nothing else occurs and time passes, those harried begin to look around and they become gradually bolder.

No man allows more than he can handle. He will gradually become too intrusive and he will be dangerous. He always thinks he can handle anything on his own, and he generally can, but the police grieve when a loner is needlessly killed.

The police in that area were aware of the odd danger. In TEXAS, they were called Rangers out in the boondocks. They are careful of the people they protect. They share in knowledge and advise the ranch crews on how to conduct themselves.

They insist on groups. Never go alone. What they should do was clear. The men were never to hesitate in calling for help. The police would rather be called and not needed, than needed and called too late.

The ranch hands kept their eyes open for intruders or any indications that somebody was crossing their land. The two pilots did flyovers with care as to seem unknowing. And word of anything odd was shared not only with the police, but with their neighbors.

And of course, the cattle rustlers were reported in a routine, rather bored manner.

The biggest gossip and knee slapping that happened was when the police hired some *rustlers* to watch for the intruders! That seemed a little like giving a honey pot to the bees. But the ex-rustlers were diligent and concerned and very good watchers! Very competitive.

It is always odd to have someone cross a line one way or the other.

The supposedly easy, self-loving Andrew still grieved for his horse. No one knew that. He would be solemn and still, looking out over the land, but always to the north and west. Mentally, he would be in a faraway land, gone.

JoAnn found him and asked, "What is it?"

He turned and frowned a little as he asked, "What?"

"You were a hundred miles away."

"No. I was thinking."

"About...what?" The trouble with minds is a woman can't see into them and know everything a man is considering. She needed to know what distracted Andrew from her. Was it a woman crossing from the house to the car lot?

How revealing that she wanted all of his attentions.

Then one day, Andrew simply vanished. JoAnn couldn't find him anywhere! She searched. She asked people on the place, "Have you seen Andrew Parsons?"

"Not for this day." That was one of the house women.

"No, not today." One of the men in the house replied.

"Nu-uh. Ya look in the house?"

"I've looked there and around the outside of the house…"

And the hand nodded seriously before he asked, "Ya wan' me to look fer 'em?"

"Please. Do you need me to tell someone you will be searching? Maybe you ought to take someone with you?"

"I'll do that."

"And tell them where you'll be searching, so's Rip can keep track?"

"I'll talk to Mr. Keeper."

"That's a good idea. Be careful."

He smiled toothlessly with a two-week beard on his scratchy chin. He told her, "I'll be careful because I know how precious I am."

"So's Andrew."

"*Ahhhh*. We'll find him."

So JoAnn went to Mrs. Keeper. "I asked one of

the crew to look for Andrew. I've searched for him
and asked everyone, but no one's seen him. He
couldn't just—vanish!''

"Don't worry, yet. We'll find him. I'll call John."

"Andrew isn't anywhere. His car's here. The horse
he rides is in the barn."

Obviously, JoAnn had searched.

Mrs. Keeper soothed, "We'll help look. Get a hat,
thin gloves and wear long sleeves, boots. We'll ride
something. Horses or pickups." Then as JoAnn
turned away, Mrs. Keeper called, "Take a gun with
you."

That caused JoAnn to pause. A gun? It could be
deadly serious. Where was Andrew?

She turned back. "I don't have a gun."

"I'll bring one for you."

JoAnn blinked. She was going to carry a gun. She
would *never* tell her mother that she had done something so rash, and that the Keepers had offhandedly
assumed that she would lug a *gun* around. How
shocking.

Carrying a gun would have to be something else
she'd never mention at home. Actually, considering
what all she had secretly overheard, or recently experienced, she wondered what all her mother had
withheld from *her* mother.

And what all secrets had been kept beyond that to
her great-grandmother? It was a shock to think any
of those gentle ladies had been sly, withholding.

It was obvious that JoAnn would have to observe
her kinswomen more closely. She would have to listen without appearing to listen. Yes.

And she looked soberly into her mirror and asked of her reflection, "Where is he?"

She was going out looking for her lover, and carrying a gun because there were people around who killed horses. Would they fire those remarkably powerful, long-distance bullets at them?

She needed to find Andrew before something terrible happened to him...and therefore...to her.

So she understood that she loved Andrew. Their experimenting hadn't been just curiosity...for her.

Had Andrew left to shed the earnest woman from his back? To lose her?

At the stables, others were mounting their horses or standing around talking. Her horse was ready. It was the one the crew had given her, and one of the crew held her horse...for her.

He smiled and held the horse steady so that she could get onto the horse. He was the one who'd been in the stable when she'd been in the hayloft with Andrew. The new, anticipating lovers had waited silently for him to leave.

Her lover. Where was Andrew?

They would look for Andrew. They would search the area and count the horses. All the trucks and cars were accounted for.

There was no question but that Andrew was out somewhere, alone and on foot.

As the riders milled, their horses eager to leave, there were crew members who brought out filled canteens with leather shoulder slings.

Sandwiches were delivered from the kitchen, and

they were put in saddlebags and probably squashed. The people were given compasses and maps. *Every*one had a compass and an area map.

A burly man who was her father's age told JoAnn, "You'll stay with me."

It was obvious to *any* one that he felt she was untried and didn't know how to use the compass or figure it out.

It was easier to monitor her entirely than it was to go out and search for another pilgrim.

He told her, "Stay close, where I can see you."

She understood him entirely and replied, "Yes." She wished for the dog Buddy. He would know where to find Andrew.

Then she thought: What if Andrew had gone to Rip's house where Buddy was staying? It was a logical walk. She mentioned this to the brusk, slightly overweight director.

With her inquiry, the older man looked at her. Then he sighed and hollered, "Call Rip's and see if Andrew is there."

Everyone was silent. They tilted their heads. They considered JoAnn. She was alert.

People dismounted and stood petting their horses' noses and mentioned things to other humans.

The talk was low. The horses were frisky. The group waited.

A houseman came out on the porch and called, "Yeah. The dog's there and so is Andrew."

Mrs. Keeper decided who of the group could stay and who was released from the gathering, but since they already carried their lunches, the rest would just go on out for a jog along the drop.

How intelligent their hostess was. If they'd had to go back inside, they'd have been disgruntled. This way, they all had an outing.

Mrs. Keeper was a smart cookie. A hostess. She knew how to smooth *anything*.

they already caused their families, the rest would just go on out for a few hours the days.

They mentioned them to ask, was, if they'd had to go back, inside, they'd have been disgruntled. This way they'd had an outing.

One man's bright strong holler: "A light at the cabin now is serious to endure—

Nine

That morning, Andrew had just gone on off, without even thinking of telling JoAnn anything at all about his leaving her there. He had given her no clue as to what he was doing or where he would be.

Andrew Parsons was supposed to be her...lover?

His disappearance had really rattled her. She'd searched *every*where and not found him. She'd been so panicked that just about the whole entire staff and guests at the Keepers had seriously gathered to search for Andrew.

They had been solemn and sober. They had listened to that middle-aged, ham-handed, very serious leader...whoever *he* was...and he'd directed who was to go which way in searching.

But with her last-minute question, as to where Andrew Parsons just might be, and the confirmation that

Andrew was, indeed, over at Rip's, the search mood had changed quite markedly.

Several of the people had kindly said to her, "I'm glad he's found."

But there were those disgusted ones who tilted back their heads and closed their eyes as they used Moses' name.

Mrs. Keeper had trained the crew to lambaste Moses instead of ticking God. God could get angry with their comments. Getting God angry wasn't worth the risk. Moses didn't have that much clout. He could handle it.

Those disgusted ones were all male. In low growls, they mentioned the lack of thinking in females.

So JoAnn went to her room, bathed and changed clothes. Then she went out and got into her car. She went on off away from the Keepers' Place, not leaving *him* any note at all. If *he* wanted *her*, he could just *look* for her and *find* her!

She knew full well, that had *she* been missing, Andrew Parsons would search by himself. It would never occur to him to gather the crowd and search. That very day, when he came back and couldn't find her, he would look for her.

If he did, it would be an intense search. Andrew could find out what disgust meant when he found her—when she reappeared—three days later—in one of the mini libraries and was calmly reading.

Meanwhile, over in the Keeper's town, Andrew was confronting Rip on Rip's own front porch. Rip came slowly over to Andrew and crowded Andrew.

Rip lifted his hand and gently tapped Andrew's chest. Rip's eyes were mean. He said, "Back off."

With logic, Andrew asked, "Is she here of her own choice?"

And Rip said, "Ask her."

So the woman who was his sister, Lu, was standing quietly on the other side of the screen door. Andrew was appalled that his sister was actually living there. But that she was all right and undisturbed did soothe her brother.

She smiled at him.

Andrew was standing on Rip's porch. Andrew limped somewhat, or perhaps more so. He had a cane. He soberly observed his sister.

Was Lu embarrassed to be found out? Andrew wondered. She seemed interested in seeing him. But she had not invited her brother inside the house. It was Rip's house. Yes.

Keeping track of Rip, Andrew saw that Rip had gotten stiff-legged. His shoulders looked bigger. His arms looked like hammers for those curled steely hands. Rip's eyes actually shot sparks.

Andrew had read of such in fiction. In this case, it was not fiction, it was real. Rip's eyes could shoot those sparks.

Without a greeting, at all, Andrew said to his sister, "I'm surprised you haven't gone on home. Do the parents know you're here?"

And *she* shrugged her shoulders and that wobbled her—chests! She smiled kindly. "They believe I'm with you, helping you recover."

"Is that so." An observation and reply with no meaning at all. No question.

She smiled in a rather sassy manner as she said, "Did daddy direct you to fetch me home?"

Andrew replied in a carefully civil way, "Our daddy has never spoken to me or given me any advice or direction."

"He's strange." She tilted her head. "Do come inside. You've met Rip. He's again taking care of your dog. Buddy arrived back here several days ago. Did you bore him into leaving you? Join us for a chat. We're about to have lunch."

For a fallen woman, she was certainly sassy and snooty. Andrew looked at Rip. Rip was dangerous. And Andrew almost began a smile as he wondered if he could...handle...Rip. Then Andrew wondered if he scared Rip. That would be interesting to know.

He asked Rip, "May I go inside?"

Rip laid it out, right away, "The dog's chosen to stay with us."

Andrew moved his head down just a tad in acknowledgment as he replied, "I understand." He said, "I've some of the dog food sacks here with me."

Lu exclaimed, "Good. He's eating all our meat."

Andrew said soberly, "You've probably ruined him."

Rip retaliated, defending Lu, "That's what the dog's eaten since I first had him."

And to prove he was adult, and that he was logical, Andrew replied, "You were very kind to take the dog in and keep him so well. I understand he flies short hops with you.''

"After I flew him out looking for you, I find he likes flying. He's a good dog.''

Andrew looked at Buddy sitting silently between the two lovers in front of Andrew. He asked the dog, "Will you come back with me?"

Buddy backed up two steps. That was clear enough. He would not go with Andrew.

Anybody that's been around them knows dogs understand human words. God was smart to keep dogs from vocally communicating. Think of all the advice and arguments God has prevented by not allowing dogs to talk human talk. It would be endlessly critical, and there would be all that advice.

This way's better.

Lu urged her brother to sit with them while they had lunch. "You're sure you don't want to share our lunch?''

"I've eaten.'' He was of the kind who could go some long time without food. He didn't want to eat at their table while he was still hostile that his sister was living with—in Rip's house.

Andrew was just about as stiff as the man of two hundred years ago that he felt he was. He watched his sister and in no time at all, he understood that the two really loved each other. So Andrew sighed and frowned a tad as he then sorted out Rip.

He asked Rip questions about flying. That was Rip's field. What would he have to say that Andrew could listen to Rip's manner of speaking? Andrew needed to probe Rip's knowledge. His future. His means in caring for a woman. Was he serious about her? Andrew set out to find out.

Actually, in spite of being a throwback to a long-ago time, the subject was current. Could Rip provide for Lu? Did he love her...enough? Really timeless questions.

Andrew sat back in his dining-room chair, at the table, and watched the two. He watched his sister smile at Rip, and he saw how vulnerable Rip was to her.

Buddy was under the table. It was obvious that the dog had chosen sides. Andrew was concerned about the dog attacking his own very vulnerable legs that were under the table. So far, to the riveted listening of the dog, Andrew's voice sounds were mature and logical.

The two lovers would never know how much the dog's intense attention to Andrew helped them. While Andrew had no real business to intrude on them at that time and chide the two, his conscience demanded that as her brother, he needed to appear profound, concerned, directive.

Rip began to relax. First because Lu accepted her brother with some delight, and second because the ponderous Andrew was logical—although he talked too much, too long. It must be stacked up conversation left over from his long, plodding adventures...without a radio. Without one, the man had too much time to think.

In their conversation, Andrew found himself adopting JoAnn's contemplation of going back in time and what she'd take to that time. Men tend to do that sort of adaptation of women's ideas. "If you were transferred back in time, what would you take with you?" he asked his sister.

Lu slid her eyes over to Rip and said, "Rip."

They touched hands and grinned at each other in a cutoff manner that excluded Andrew entirely. So he said, "What utensils. What would be important to you to have along?" And he added with some endurance, "—besides Rip."

The lovers shared their laugh.

Try as he did, Andrew didn't really get anything meaningful from the two. They were in La-la land. They were cheerful and reasonably courteous, but actually they mostly ignored Andrew.

Even the dog ignored Andrew. The visit was saddening. He meant nothing to any of them, at all. Lu had been raised to be courteous and she skimmed along the edge of that manner.

Outside of deadly looks that would shrivel Andrew into backing off, Rip tended to ignore the guest altogether.

They wouldn't always be thataway. Andrew asked the pair, "Have you quarreled as yet?"

"Endlessly." That was Rip as he smiled at the flower who was Lu.

Lu explained, "He wanted me to cook." She laughed over that one.

Rip replied, "She learned."

Lu bragged, "I make all sorts of...toast...and I can open...*cans!*"

Rip's laughter was along with hers.

Under the table, the dog was silent. Andrew still

had whole, unbloodied ankles. There are times when such is a plus.

Would Buddy ever come back to him? Andrew wondered. But he was smart enough not to try to lure his dog out from under the table. The dog's being there, hidden, was a clue that the dog felt he'd vanished.

How sad.

The dog probably felt he was the only real defense of the two he'd chosen.

And Andrew remembered a time back a way that he'd been ill and lying—about dead—in his blankets by a low fire, at night, and the wolves came. Buddy had held them back with snarls and attacks. He was a good dog.

When Andrew finally rose to leave, Lu came to him and hugged him. He looked beyond to Rip who wasn't as committed to Andrew as he was to Andrew's sister. Rip was territorial. He wanted Lu. He was courteous and shook hands, but he hadn't accepted Andrew as kin…yet.

Andrew allowed his ex-dog to be silent and hidden.

He left, carefully using the cane and strode back to the ranch house just a while away. No one seemed to be around. JoAnn wasn't in her room, and Andrew couldn't find her. He finally asked one of the cleaning women.

She replied, "I'll call Clara. She helped Miss Murray pack."

Pack? Andrew's entire body system became rigid. Pack? Leave? To where?

So Clara showed up and smiled as she—

"Where is JoAnn Murray?"

"She went to visit a friend out east, as I recall. She talked to Mrs. Keeper."

Andrew walked on off, just like that. He burst into Mrs. Keeper's office and asked everybody there, "Where is JoAnn Murray?"

And Mrs. Keeper replied by herself, "She's gone to a friend's house for a card party?" The TEXAS do-you-understand questioning statement. "I believe it was a bridge tournament."

"Where." Not even a question. Just a demand.

"I don't believe she mentioned that, but some of her clothes are still here. She'll be back."

"When?"

"Dear boy, I have no idea. I didn't speak with her. She just wrote a note and left. It must have been sudden. With bridge, that way, it could have been a last minute fill-in."

"Did she leave a note for me?"

"Not that I recall. Have you looked in your room?"

He actually left without replying. That made Mrs. Keeper smile and raise her eyebrows at her secretary.

But Andrew found there was no note there from JoAnn in his room. No note...nothing. He was sundered. She was his!

How could she leave so carelessly? He thought that as he hunted down the cleaning crew and made them go through all the wastebasket trash to be sure there hadn't been a note for him from her.

There was none.

Rosco told Andrew with naked eyes, "We don't

never throw away anybody's notes even if they're three weeks laying around. If they're not crumpled up and torn up and put in the wastebasket, we don't touch nothing that's a note or a letter. We know better.''

"Do you know where she went?''

Rosco inquired carefully, "Who?''

"Miss Murray.''

"That one. Nope. We didn't pay no mind.'' He turned aside and hollered, "Hey! Nick?''

There was a negative reply. That one called back. "He ain't here. Want him?''

And Rosco replied, "Yeah. Get him.'' Then he said to Andrew. "If there's anybody that notices *any*thing, it's Nick. We'll talk to him.''

And Andrew said— He actually *said,* "Thank you.''

While that didn't waggle Rosco, at all, it should have. It was the first time in Andrew's whole, entire life that he'd voluntarily said the words. That probably showed he was earnest and really needed the information.

What had ever boggled Andrew before then?— other than his father. His costudents in England?

Nick was found. He came with some interest and curiosity. Andrew was talked about in the crew. He was...different. He'd been an asinine clod in demanding that he be waited on by the crew. They'd fixed that. But it'd taken Mrs. Keeper to help them straighten him out.

So Nick was careful and very relaxed. He'd have to hear what this pilgrim wanted.

So Andrew asked, "Nick, do you know anything about Miss Murray leaving and why?"

"She said she'd be back in a couple of days. That was about all we ever heard. She just took one bag, but none of us knows where all she went. Did you ask Mrs. Keeper?"

"She suggested that I contact you all. She didn't know."

It was then Andrew caught their attention. They studied him. He was silent as he looked thoughtfully out a window. He mentioned, "Women are strange."

The men laughed but the one woman was huffy. She said, "It's *men* who louse up this planet!"

Andrew considered her. "You may be right." He said it kindly. It wasn't what he *should* have said, but it was better than what he might have said.

In the three days that he waited, Andrew had a lot to think about. Actually it wasn't really three— whole—days. The lapse in time just went to the third day. It was very similar to his being trapped under his horse.

That whole, entire time, Andrew paced the wide, shaded front porch of the Keepers' house. Or he sat on one of the lounge chairs. It was not extended, it was rigidly upright so that he could see down the driveway as far as was possible.

Why her?

Why was he so triggered by that JoAnn Murray? And her image cleared in his mind. It'd been there all along anyway, now he really looked at her. In his mind, he watched her flirt and laugh. He saw her reading a book and looking up at him in a discarding manner.

He saw her looking around outside, as they walked, with her hair blowing around the edges of her hat. He watched her walk and place her feet one at a time in the jumble that was the dish of cacti and rocks and scrubby trees.

His mind watched her speak to other people. And he saw her face as she looked at him. He saw the straw in her hair after he'd made love to her in the stable.

She was magic.

Why had she left him without any note or call or contact? That bothered him especially. It was some time before his mind mentioned that he had left the Keepers' house and walked into the little town to see his sister. He hadn't left a message for JoAnn, telling her where he'd be and why.

It was his own stupidity that caused all this tension! It was a lesson to himself. He needed better communication.

He did not want to be like his useless father.

That was especially catching to Andrew. If he wasn't to be *like* his father, then he needed to…communicate with other people. Be a part of them.

So he didn't ring the bell for help, he got up and went into the house and found the library. There he found a pad, a pencil and an envelope.

He took those things out to the porch and surveyed the entrance road yet again. It was empty. Well, there was the man who mowed the lawn and that man's woman who trimmed things—precisely. There were dogs out and about.

He missed Buddy.

Then he went on looking and realized how *busy* it all was. He'd never before seen how very *busy* everybody was!

He was not.

He walked or sat. He had no involvement in anything else. Just...himself. How odd to realize that.

So he wrote a letter to his father and asked questions. How could he guide his life better? How could he mean something to *this* time? And he told his father about JoAnn.

Then he tore that all up and just wrote as to where he was and that he planned to go to the yearly gathering at his old school in England.

Now, that was interesting. Why in this *world* would he want to go to a place he had so badly wanted to leave?

He spent some time considering that, and understood that it had been the only nurturing he'd ever received. He'd been just like most of those other boys, removed from families and allowed to be taught and disciplined by experts.

Then Andrew began to remember what all he'd learned at that strict place. The manners, the discipline, the learning of how to cope with anything.

He *knew* how to cope. He'd been *taught* to be in charge. He did not need to try to punish his father any longer.

Ahhhhh. So that had been his problem. And Andrew sat and considered what an ass he'd been in trying to catch his mother's sole attention.

For a man of his age, he was a little slow in learning. In understanding. He would take JoAnn to England for the reunion of all the scholars. How many would he know? How many of his teachers would still be there?

He could at least show someone else where he'd been and what it'd been like there. And he gradually realized what all he'd been taught. That patience, the care, the molding of him that he'd rejected...until now.

—and he finally faced the fact that *he* had not been rejected by the students there, it was he who had rejected the approaches of the other boys.

Andrew had only been rejected by his own father.

His whole life had been in rebellion of his father. He'd deliberately not mixed with the others because he was so jealous of his mother being entirely claimed by his father. And he'd allowed that to rule his stupid life.

The rejection of today was going back two hundred years, riding a horse and being asinine. He really was a jackass.

Because of his concern for JoAnn, Andrew had had the time to sit and watch for her, and in that unused time, he'd begun to understand his own life.

He would go to England for the reunion. Who would he know? And he thought back and remembered faces.

As Andrew sat there, he began to remember names. Names of his teachers, names of his classmates. There was the snaggletoothed, uh, Trevor! By golly, Andrew wondered, would Trevor be there? Trevor... what? And he got out a small leather book and opened it to a clean page.

He finally had five names...and her car came up the winding driveway.

JoAnn was there.

Andrew put the small, leather book into his pocket as he stood up.

She looked at him coldly out of the car window—and she drove on back to the garage.

So Andrew went around the house and followed. She was already in the garage when he arrived. She was climbing out of the car. She slammed the door. She didn't look at him. She opened the trunk, and he reached past her for her suitcase.

She said, "I can carry it. Give it to me."

"I beg your pardon for not telling you where I would be. I went to see my sister over in the town. She really loves Rip. I don't believe you've been up in Rip's plane to look at the land with him, have you?"

He was acting like they were friends? She was offended and irritated. But he walked beside her carrying her case...and he talked.

He had asked pardon and told her of going to Rip's and why. Would she forgive him?

She looked at him. That was why she'd left some of her clothes here. She had wanted another look at this creature.

He could easily tell that she was still angry. But she wasn't shouting at him, or swinging her purse at his head, nor was she refusing to walk alongside of him.

He asked, "How did the game go?"

"The game?"

"Wasn't it a bridge marathon that you were dragged to to fill the empty chair of someone else?"

That surprised her. "Yes."

"How did it go?"

JoAnn wondered, when had he ever wanted information from someone else? He'd only talked about himself. He was interesting, but he was very much interested only in himself.

This was a breakthrough? She looked at Andrew. He smiled at her. He said, "I was afraid you wouldn't come back. I searched for you everywhere and even made the crew let me go through all the day's trash so that I could know you did not leave me a note when you left. Why didn't you? I was sundered."

He'd *noticed* she was gone? He was upset that she was? She said, "Since you left no note as to where you were, I didn't think you'd care where I was."

Andrew stopped and took her against him. JoAnn was a bit stiffened. He told her in a low voice, "I was afraid you wouldn't come back. I didn't know where to find you. They said you weren't at your home."

And she began to understand him. Or—was it just sex. Men do tend to try to keep some handy woman around for that.

He said, "Come with me. It's been at least a year since I've seen you." He smiled down at her so kindly with shared humor.

But she wasn't lured especially. The bridge game had been dead heat and serious. Some women are thataway. It had been hell-bent the whole entire time!

She said, "I'm exhausted."

"I know exactly how to relax you. I've played cut-throat bridge myself. I can save you." He grinned and his eyes danced.

And she said, "Baloney."

He lifted his hands. "You're assuming wrong. This is a rubdown that loosens tired muscles and allows you to sleep. Let me."

That "Let me" was suspect. She allowed him to turn her and she went along, he opened the door for her to enter the house.

There was not one person anywhere around—at all—in their whole, entire trip to his room.

She asked logically, "Why are we in your room and not mine?"

"I have the ointment here." He said that. He smiled kindly. He suggested, "Would you like to strip in the bath? You can take this towel with you. Or...I could help you."

His concern was open and gentle and very, very sly.

She inquired, "Has this worked very often?"

"I've never before tried it. Which way will it be? I'm harmless."

Those last two words made her eyes dance. She said, "Harmless." She tasted that word as she watched him. Then she said, "Of course."

He said, "After that bridge tournament, remembering all those cards and who played what how and when, you must feel a bit hyper and tense. You need to relax. There is an ancient Middle Eastern massage that relaxes someone that tense. Let me help you.''

She coughed rather fakely. It would have been to cover a laugh? And she bit her lower lip.

He took off his shirt and trousers. He slid out of his shoes and left his socks on because they wouldn't interfere. He explained before she could question. ''Helping someone else relax is hard work, and I sweat.''

Sure.

So she did allow him to undress her. She was curious just how he would...handle all this and exactly how he'd manipulate her...how—practiced—he was.

He was either dead stupid or a hambone. He was awkward. He tried to get her skirt off without unzipping it. He pulled her shirt off over her head and it caught, because it wasn't unbuttoned. He was really inept.

Or...he was remarkably sly.

Ten

For a man of Andrew's age, it was interesting for JoAnn to witness his remarkable lack of knowing the handling of a woman. He was so earnest and careful. He breathed oddly.

It was supposed to be from exertion, not lust.

He struggled so well to get the garments off JoAnn. Andrew was earnest. He had to wrestle with *every*-thing on her. He acted as if he'd never done it before. At his age?

Well, *may*be the woman had disrobed herself? Saved him the time? Been eager? JoAnn turned jealous. She asked, "How many women have you un-dressed?" And she lifted her eyebrows gently as she waited for his reply.

Andrew looked at her blankly. He considered. He frowned. He asked, "Am I all that bad at it?"

"You appear to be quite engrossed."

"Engrossed." He frowned as he thought about it. "I'm gross?"

"No. You're awkward."

"Well, I *could* go out and find somebody in the crew who could get this done, but I—hush—I hesitate to allow anybody else to put his hands on—your clothing." Andrew waited a tad and then explained, "Their hands might not be clean."

She laughed. She looked at him. She was amused by him. She became more tolerant. She asked, "Shall I help?"

"No. This is my job. I'm soothing you."

"You're wrecking my hair."

He looked at her head of mussed-up hair very seriously evaluating it. "It looks fine. A little tumbled, but okay." His male hands smoothed her hair. He pulled it straight down and along her head as he "neated" it. Yes.

Fortunately, JoAnn was not at all insufferably aware of her hair or how it was on her head. She felt pretty anyway, and which way her hair was blown or moved was of no real interest to her.

JoAnn watched him.

He was judging her hair. He said, "You're a good-looking woman."

"Thank you."

He shrugged. "I didn't have any part in making you thataway."

She was patient. "I was expressing a courtesy for your compliment."

"You like being pretty?"

"I never noticed."

Andrew laughed. He laughed with such humor, so filled by it that he looked at her to share it with her.

She was patiently tolerant.

He said, "I'm gonna git you."

"You've already had me. Another time would not be a surprise."

In some shock, he inquired, "Didn't you think I was any good at all?"

"You did well. I suppose. I've not had anyone with whom I could compare you."

"You've held out all this time? How'd you manage that?"

And she replied, "I lock my door."

"If you were that pristine, how come you did it with me?"

"I was curious."

He smiled. "Curious...about me and how I would be?"

"How it would be...for me."

"Oh." He looked at her with naked eyes. "Wasn't I any good?" How else would a discarded man in time inquire such?

He surprised JoAnn. He hadn't known how good he was? How he'd waited and manipulated her? He hadn't—used—her, he'd shared.

She was honest, "You're obviously very good. I can't tell if you're better than any other man because I haven't had that experience. You were my first and—"

"Your...first." Andrew considered. "You sure

took to it with a whole lot of effort! You scared the hell out of me. I figured you knew more than I did.''

''Not likely.''

And he questioned, ''Why…not…likely? Was I that bad?''

''You're not bad,'' she explained, ''but you're most certainly wicked. I was so excited and surprised and wanted you so mu—''

''You *wanted* me?''

''Didn't you notice?''

''You drove me crazy! You were so quick and so eager that I was excited right out of my head.''

And *she* said, ''Let's do that again.''

Andrew gasped. His eyes looked into space. He said, ''I think I'm going into overdrive. I've heard guys talk about that. What if I pass out? Can you get out from under me okay?''

And with her eyes at half-mast, JoAnn smiled— wickedly! And she *said* to Andrew, ''We'll see.''

Now what is a man to do under those circumstances? Andrew said, ''You terrify me. How can you be this calm and experimenting when I know good and well I was your first.''

''So I wasn't *your* first?''

''No. One of the cleaning ladies in England showed me the ropes. I was in bed with the flu, and she felt sorry for me—she said.''

''What did you do?''

''I was…fascinated. I suppose if my fever hadn't been so high, I might have, uh, declined, but I wasn't really in touch. Not aware, that is. She was touching me! And old Freeman didn't mind at all.''

"Ahhhhh."

"Will you go with me to England?"

JoAnn squinted and asked, "Why would I do that?"

"You're bringing me up to time. This isn't at all easy for me. My father sent me off to school, and I've never been back or invited back. I was always told to travel or to search for my own kind of life. I haven't gone back home."

"How strange."

"I watch the Keepers and wonder how it would have been for me if my family had been around me thisaway."

JoAnn said, "I believe you've done very well. You *do* need more help in undressing a female body, but you're determined and don't give up. That's a plus. I would suggest that you learn to be more gentle with her clothes. You need to realize there are buttons and zippers."

"*Her* clothes? Who else did you have in mind for me?" Andrew was somewhat appalled.

"No one. I just thought you needed some guidance."

"Have you suspected that I want you?"

"There's been a hint or two."

"How'd you know?"

"You kissed me."

He was a tad indignant. "Not when I began to strip you?"

"That was the time element. Your kiss was not a hello kiss, it was a we're-gonna-do-it kiss."

"I hadn't realized I was that smart."

"You were intense."

He nodded. "Yeah. I felt pretty focused."

She laughed in a helpless manner.

Andrew watched her. He groaned. He slid alongside of her. He kissed her witless.

She gasped and rubbed against him. She looked at him rather triggered. His eyes were hot. She said, "Do it."

And *he* said, "I thought I'd just lay back, being this tired from trying to get you out of your clothes and all. And you can do it to me." He smiled.

But his eyes were busy and hot, and he had to lick his lips and swallow, but he could do all that without letting go of her.

She said, "Lie back and be quiet."

He lay back rather avidly, his breaths too fast and his pulse pounding rather obviously. Very quietly, he whispered, "Help! Help!"

She said a raucously naughty, "Hah! Gotcha!"

And as he whimpered and gasped and carried on outrageously *and* gave directions, she used his body and rode him down.

It was just about too quick.

She collapsed on him, and he could feel her heart thundering along with his own. He was very touched by her wanting him. He kissed her cheek. He lifted her hand to his mouth and pressed his lips to her hand. His other hand smoothed back her hair.

Her eyes were closed and she was lax on top of his body. Her mouth smiled and she said a whole lot of "Ummmmmmm's."

* * *

Their departure from the Keepers was not subtle. They told everyone goodbye with charming courtesy. They told the Keepers where they would be in England. They thanked the crew and gave out envelopes to those who'd helped them with directions or mending or cleaning clothing. They bragged on the kitchen crew and saluted them, leaving an envelope there to be shared. It had been a lovely time. Envelopes had been left in their rooms for the cleanup crew.

With fond goodbyes, they went out and got into JoAnn's car. She drove. Andrew didn't mind at all. He could look at her. His smile never left his face. He said, "I can't believe I've found you."

And being truthful, she replied, "Mrs. Keeper asked me to come to their place so that I could find you a wife."

He laughed.

"Now...why...is that amusing?"

"I got you."

"Isn't it amazing? You were so snotty and aloof. I was there to smooth you out and—"

"You did that, I'm like a rubber man who has no innards, at all."

She looked over at him for an instant before she finished her sentence, "—find you a wife."

"I think you'll do just right."

She didn't take her eyes off the road but she exclaimed, "You're talking TEXAN!"

He explained ponderously, "A man has many facets."

"Oh? And a woman?"

"—has a fine body."

She sighed with great patience. "But her mind is more astute."

"There's a tree along the road up ahead. Let's pull off behind it."

"No. You'd just get me all sticky and messed up and I'd have to either remember to first take off my lipstick or I'd look like I'd been slurping a raspberry Popsicle."

He suggested kindly, "I'd lick it off."

"Don't lure me."

Watching her, Andrew asked, "Are you lured?"

"For one reason or another, you make my blood pump quite shockingly."

"Wanna know what you do to Freeman?"

JoAnn cautioned, "Not when I'm driving." Then she gave him a quick, seeing glance, as she turned back to watch the road, she asked, "How come you're talking entirely different now."

"It's all the places I've been. I can talk England or I can talk TEXAS."

"Where would you prefer to be?"

"With you."

"That was very courteous of you, but what is the actual reply? Where do you want to be?"

"I've lived a very strange life. I'll take you to England and I'll take you to meet my parents. You can help me decide."

JoAnn told him, "There is no way, at all, that you could bend to someone else's directions."

"I'm pliant."

She drove a ways considering, and then she said, "We'll see."

* * *

So they flew to England for the reunion gathering of the summer. The varying classes were mostly in separate areas, so Andrew did find his group. He and JoAnn shared a student's room. They went to dinner and the entire ritual was so familiar to Andrew.

He remembered names. That is a plus. He introduced those he knew to JoAnn. And they were all charming, but the remarkable thing was, they remembered *him!*

They said, "Old boy..." They said, "TEXAN." Andrew had forgotten how many times they'd called him a Yank. He'd trained them to say TEXAN. They loved still saying it. They were courteous and kind, and they were especially kind to JoAnn.

Andrew said, "She's mine." He said, "Back off." He said, "She is not a kissing cousin."

The men all protested that anyone who lived together the long time they had, were cousins! Hadn't he realized that? And cousins *always* hugged and kissed if they were female.

Andrew licked his smile and said, "She was not here in class. I brought her along to see this place. You may not kiss her."

They protested they could not be so rude! She had come to their land and they felt welcoming.

Andrew warned casually, "Down, boy."

And they howled like dogs.

Of course, they asked Andrew what all he was doing, and they listened. And they told what they were about, and Andrew listened. And it was only then that he recalled how formally kind they had been with the bitter Andrew of long ago.

He had been determined to not like any of the time there in England as a reject of his father. Andrew had done that. He had rejected his father entirely because he hadn't wanted the opportunity of having the experience his father had wanted for him.

Andrew looked around. He *saw* the place with open eyes. He remembered many things that were kind and carefully done for him by faculty and particularly by his age group. And he remembered other English boys who'd been homesick and unhappy.

Andrew was not only ordinary in his manners, he was one of them. How strange to understand, after all those years, that he had been well treated and well taught.

It had been his own doing that had made him bitter. How different his life would have been had he just adjusted and learned.

Think of all the young men and older men who went to war and were bored most of the time. Think of those who spent lax time digging their tunnels out of prison areas, and being caught and taken back. It kept them busy. They *did* something! They didn't just sit and rot.

And Andrew considered how he'd participated in all the games and in all the classes at that school. He'd forgotten all that. He'd remembered only the bitter parts. How stupid of him.

"I liked it here." He mentioned that one evening to JoAnn.

She nodded. "It is such a charming place. You can

see beyond.'' And she looked at the countryside, which was so peaceful and green, so prettily kept. ''Who started this place here?''

''Next to England, the U.S.A. is a budding place.'' He replied, ''This school was started long, long ago.''

''The buildings are so formal. It's nice.''

Andrew remembered that, even back then, he'd noticed the area. Why had his unhappiness covered it all? In going to school there, it had been—special. It was a beautiful place. The people he'd known there had been kind. Why were his memories so bitter?

Just because his father had sent him away? How dumb to have allowed that to interfere with his life. It was a waste of time. It was selfish. He remembered returning from Europe and his grandmother in exasperation saying to his complaints, ''Oh, go nurse the lepers.''

She meant that there are others who need help and he did not.

She'd been right. He was the nerd. Why had he taken so long to understand that? And Andrew looked over at JoAnn. How strange to understand how smart she was to drag him out of his cocoon.

—or had he finally grown up on his own when he lay those almost three whole days under a dead horse and gradually realized he had no place to go?

He could do whatever he wanted to do. He was free of his bitterness toward his father. He understood he'd had a remarkable adventure in England and in traveling.

And he finally realized, it was his choice to go home and see his father. He had not been rejected, it was he who was punishing them. How stupid. Really stupid.

He looked at JoAnn. "When we get back to the States, would you go with me to meet my family?" And even in saying that, he knew if she could not go then, he could go by himself. He needed no crutch.

He was released from his own, self-made prison! He looked around, outside of himself. He was no longer bound by self-deception. He was free.

He said to JoAnn, "I care about you."

"It's too soon."

"Too soon?"

She shrugged. "We don't know each other well enough as yet. We'll see."

He smiled at her. He realized she was right. He was out of his shell and he ought to look around and be sure. They had only known each other less than a month.

Andrew watched JoAnn. How had he managed to really see her? He'd been a real snot. It was she who'd led him into listening and realizing that it was good to be with another person and share what was going on. It was her patience that had finally managed to get him to open up and pay attention.

Andrew hadn't gotten out of his shell, by himself. It was she who had forced it open. Only then did he begin to understand the Keepers.

With the reunion over, the two visitors went to London. They went to the squares. They went to the museum and saw the black stone, which held the language of long ago. It was what the curious ones had found to understand the languages, for each was the same communication and, knowing only one, they could then decipher the other language. A miracle stone.

Who had been the brilliant ones who'd thought that far ahead to another time...to communicate with other peoples? It didn't matter who they were but what they'd thought to do.

The two visitors saw Trafalgar Square and the pigeons there. They strolled in Queen's Gate in Hyde Park. They stayed on the path. There were the theaters, the monuments, the wonderful city, the changing of the guards and they were charmed by it all. They listened to the people and saw how similar we are. No wonder.

They left their hotel with their luggage and took a train to cross to the west coast of the bottom of England. There they went by ferry to Ireland and took a tourist bus along the way and watched and saw.

So from Ireland, the two adventurers flew back to the States. And they took another flight down to Houston. As they left the plane, he questioned JoAnn, "Come along and meet my people?"

"Have you called them, as yet?"

He had not. He was still partially in his I'm-in-control lock. He smiled and slowly nodded his head a tad in recognition as he said to her, "I'll call."

It was his mother who answered the phone.

He said, "This is your son, Andrew. I've—"

"Are you all right?"

"Of course. JoAnn and I—"

"JoAnn? Are you married?"

"Not yet. We are just back from England, and we wondered if you're free so that we can come—"

"Yes!"

"We're looking forward to seeing you. What time would be conve—"

"Now!""

So they took a cab and rode out to his old house. It was lovely to see. His mother was out the door and running to them with her arms out.

Andrew gave the money to JoAnn to pay the cab-driver and caught his mother just in time.

His mother exclaimed and hugged him and tears leaked from her eyes as she laughed.

By then, the cab was gone.

Mrs. Parsons's tears were glad ones and she finally released Andrew and hugged JoAnn. And exclaiming, she walked between them and took their hands. She was exuberant that they were there.

Andrew really didn't have to say much.

They went into the house, and his father was standing back enough for them to clear the door. The two men shook hands but Mr. Parsons gently hugged his son.

That felt so odd to Andrew. He stepped back and introduced his father to JoAnn.

Mr. Parsons put one hand on her shoulder as he shook her other hand. "I'm so glad to see you."

He said that to JoAnn but he looked at Andrew. He said, "You've grown up."

And Andrew replied soberly, "Just recently."

It was a tear-damp time. The four sat and talked.

His mother and father and Andrew did the talking. JoAnn listened. Her eyes were watery.

Andrew's father said, "Mrs. Keeper kept us informed about your time in the hospital. And we heard from Lu quite faithfully. She was so kind to go there and stay. Where is she now?"

"She's still out there on the Keepers' Place."

"How come she didn't come on home when you got better?"

"She's involved."

"Oh?"

"She's met a flyer and she cottons to him. We'll see how it goes."

"Is she staying with you?"

And he adjusted that as he said, "At the Keepers'."

His mother said, "Stay with us."

Andrew looked at JoAnn and he raised his eyebrows. This visit was not on her list.

She shrugged and allowed him to decide. So he asked JoAnn, "Tonight?"

His mother asked, "This week?"

JoAnn said, "Two days."

So the two did stay with the senior Parsons. It was interesting. The visiting lovers had separate rooms. The two smiled at each other and were mature enough that they could handle being separated at night.

But knowing parents, JoAnn had limited their separation to just two nights.

Being with Mr. Parsons was a whole lot like being with Andrew. They were of the same ilk.

Andrew might change enough that he would leave

the cloak of his father behind. Andrew might very well become logical. How interesting that would be. He was like a turtle.

JoAnn considered the label and realized it was true. Andrew was only now pushing his head out from under his shell and looking around to see the world... and beyond.

Soon he just might stretch his neck out into the open and swing his head around to see other things, farther away.

He might even leave that protective encasing and stride out with greater interest.

It would be interesting to watch.

JoAnn would ask Mrs. Keeper how to help Andrew to spread his wings...and fly!

The two lovers returned to the Keepers' as if they were a part of them. Their rooms were still theirs. The Keepers were remarkable. They'd be welcoming if the people who left would return and be without space.

Was that automatic? Or was it because the Keepers had been there so long that the courtesy just continued. Who knew when guests would return? That probably was started several hundred years ago when the Keepers had guests who had no real place to go in that new land?

To them it was new. It had been different from Europe, but people had already been on these two lost continents for many and many a century.

At the Keepers', Andrew assumed his room would still be his, and he went there.

JoAnn inquired of Mrs. Keeper's secretary, "Do you know if I have a room?"

The secretary blinked. "We always keep rooms ready for a month after people leave. They generally come back."

And JoAnn mentioned, "If I didn't have a place to stay, here, I could bunk with Andrew."

The secretary blinked and observed JoAnn for a blank minute. Then she smiled. Then she said in sassy humor, "I'm so sorry. We've used your room for another guest. We're just about filled up, but Andrew *does* have two beds in his room. Shall I inquire if he would mind a roomie?"

"I'll tell him." JoAnn smiled a cat's smile and left.

Andrew wasn't in his room. His luggage was piled in a small mound. He hadn't even bothered to unpack. Where was he? Gone to see his absent dog? Gone to tell his sister about his parents? Just...gone?

Without a word to her, he'd left.

That made JoAnn feel sad. She wasn't prime for him. She was a convenience? Just convenient.

She ought to lea—

And the door opened. It was, indeed, Andrew. His face bare, he looked at her. "I looked *every*where for you. You weren't in your room. I looked for your car. It was there in the garage. But I couldn't find *you!*"

"We need to communicate."

"My God, I thought I'd lost you again."

"You haven't ever lost me, how could it be—again?"

"You've given up on me a couple of times. You're

the one who has brought me out of my shell." He was not talking about turtle shells.

JoAnn watched with great interest. "You love me."

"How could you not know that?" He was somewhat indignant.

"You don't mention love."

"I took you to England with me so that you could see where I'd been."

"Just you. Not the people who were there?"

"I didn't know if they would be back or which of the staff was still around. It's been a long time since I was there."

"They knew you."

"Yes." He admitted that but his entire attention was on her. He told her, "I'd die if you left me now."

"I can—leave you—later?"

He was intense. He admitted, "Probably...never."

"I'll consider it."

"Soon. I don't want to hassle you or follow you or hold on to your dress so that you don't leave me. I need to know if I wake up, you'll be there."

"I would never sneak out. I would tell you first."

Andrew questioned, "Would you listen to any arguments opposing your leaving?"

JoAnn replied, "Well, we can hardly stay here all the rest of our lives."

He considered that. "I hadn't thought about that. I'd only thought about you being with me—somewhere. And since we're now here, I assumed it would be here."

She suggested, "We might rent one of the houses the crew has a couple of blocks away from here."

"I rather like it here."

"The servants?"

"It is convenient."

JoAnn inquired with interest. "What are you like without servants?"

He watched her. He said carefully, "I can learn anything."

"Chopping wood?"

Andrew nodded. "I've done that. I've traveled by horse and I've learned to fix camps."

"You should write a book or so."

Andrew replied thoughtfully, "I could."

And she shrugged. "Why not?"

He told her, "I do have an income. We could be wherever you might want to be."

"—with you."

That melted him altogether. He said, "JoAnn..." It was just her name. He watched her. "Do you realize how important you've been to me? How much I love you?"

JoAnn clarified it all, "You're only surfacing. You need to be sure this is important to you. I am a woman. You know I've not been with any other man. I love you, but you could ruin me."

"We'll take it easy. I'll have the time to convince you. We can find a place to be together. I love you."

"We'll see."

He smiled. "I've heard that all my life. And we always do—see whatever it is. Trust me."

She put her hand in his outstretched one and she moved closer to him, but he met her halfway.

And that's the way their lives went on. They met halfway, and they worked to understand each other. It was true love.

* * * * *

*Be sure to look for Tom's story,
the next installment of*
THE KEEPERS OF TEXAS *Series,
available in September from Silhouette Desire.
This book will also mark Lass Small's
50th title for Silhouette!*

Take 2 bestselling love stories FREE

Plus get a FREE surprise gift!

Special Limited-Time Offer

Mail to Silhouette Reader Service™

P.O. Box 609
Fort Erie, Ontario
L2A 5X3

YES! Please send me 2 free Silhouette Desire® novels and my free surprise gift. Then send me 6 brand-new novels every month, which I will receive months before they appear in bookstores. Bill me at the low price of $3.49 each plus 25¢ delivery and GST*. That's the complete price, and a saving of over 10% off the cover prices—quite a bargain! I understand that accepting the books and gift places me under no obligation ever to buy any books. I can always return a shipment and cancel at any time. Even if I never buy another book from Silhouette, the 2 free books and the surprise gift are mine to keep forever.

326 SEN CH7V

Name	(PLEASE PRINT)
Address	Apt. No.
City	Province	Postal Code

This offer is limited to one order per household and not valid to present Silhouette Desire® subscribers. *Terms and prices are subject to change without notice. Canadian residents will be charged applicable provincial taxes and GST.

CDES-98 ©1990 Harlequin Enterprises Limited

MARILYN PAPPANO

Concludes the twelve-book series— 36 Hours—in June 1998 with the final installment

YOU MUST REMEMBER THIS

Who was "Martin Smith"? The sexy stranger had swept into town in the midst of catastrophe, with no name and no clue to his past. Shy, innocent Julie Crandall found herself fascinated—and willing to risk everything to be by his side. But as the shocking truth regarding his identity began to emerge, Julie couldn't help but wonder if the *real* man would prove simply too hot to handle.

For Martin and Julie and *all* the residents of Grand Springs, Colorado, the storm-induced blackout had been just the beginning of 36 Hours that changed *everything*—and guaranteed a lifetime forecast of happiness for twelve very special couples.

Available at your favorite retail outlet.

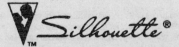

Silhouette®

The World's Most Eligible Bachelors are about to be named! And Silhouette Books brings them to you in an all-new, original series....

World's Most
Eligible Bachelors

Twelve of the sexiest, most sought-after men share every intimate detail of their lives in twelve never-before-published novels by the genre's top authors.

Don't miss these unforgettable stories by:

Dixie Browning

MARIE FERRARELLA

Jackie Merritt

Tracy Sinclair

BJ James

RACHEL LEE

Suzanne Carey

Gina Wilkins

VICTORIA PADE

MAGGIE SHAYNE

Anne McAllister

Susan Mallery

Look for one new book each month in the
World's Most Eligible Bachelors series beginning
September 1998 from Silhouette Books.

V™ *Silhouette*®

Available at your favorite retail outlet.

Look us up on-line at: http://www.romance.net   PSWMEB

MATERNITY LEAVE

Coming September 1998

Three delightful stories about the blessings
and surprises of "Labor" Day.

TABLOID BABY by Candace Camp

She was whisked to the hospital in the nick of time....

THE NINE-MONTH KNIGHT
by Cait London

A down-on-her-luck secretary is experiencing
odd little midnight cravings....

THE PATERNITY TEST by Sherryl Woods

The stick turned blue before her
biological clock struck twelve....

*These three special women are very pregnant...and very
single, although they won't be either for too much longer,
because baby—and Daddy—are on their way!*

Available at your favorite retail outlet.

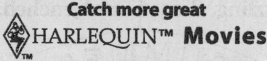

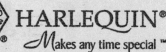